THE LAVENDER HOUSE IN MEUSE

GAIL NOBLE-SANDERSON

Noble
Press

Other books by Gail Noble-Sanderson
The Passage Home to Meuse

THE LAVENDER HOUSE IN MEUSE

Published by Noble Press LLC
Mount Vernon, Washington
gnoble_sanderson@comcast.net

Author Photo by Travis Christians Photography
Cover Art by Kathleen Noble
Cover design and typesetting by Enterline Design Services

ISBN: 978-0-9991386-2-5
Library of Congress Control Number: pending

Printed in the United States of America

*This book is dedicated to all those who care
for the wounded.*

*They say a mother's love is powerful beyond what can be imagined—
that it transcends all time. Losing you once, Maman, as you gave me
life, I find you now as you give me life once again.*

Our memories, like love, transcend all time.

TABLE OF CONTENTS

FROM THE AUTHOR

Some years ago, as everyone around me became enthralled with all things lavender—extolling its health benefits and how its very sight and smell prompted positive feelings of calm and contentment—I was simply puzzled. Even a hint of the fragrance from a pretty ribbon-tied bunch of lavender in a quaint shop would send me close to tears, feelings of sadness rolling over and over me.

Yet somehow, I was continually drawn to lavender. The purple periwinkle color had always been my favorite, and I appreciated the many varieties of the plant itself. Certainly here in the Pacific Northwest lavender graced many a garden. Growing in someone else's garden was fine—just not my own. Tulips and daffodils made me happy, but I held no desire to add anything lavender to my blooms.

During this same time period, beginning around 1994, I would wake up in the early morning conscious that I had not been merely dreaming but was instead experiencing some type of vivid memory. The memories of a young soldier named Laurent came first. I could describe in great detail the bedroom he slept in, saw the pale yellow curtains fluttering around his open window, and was taken over by grief at his hardship.

This memory of Laurent was recurring and became so familiar that I was eventually able to separate my feelings and begin to pay attention to details and explore the memory. I could easily recall more of this place I saw so clearly in my mind. I was in a house, and there were other injured men in this house with me. In my mind, I could walk through all the rooms and experience every detail of light, texture, and smell. Walking out the back door or looking through the window at the top of the landing, I could see rolling fields of lavender. Out the front door, I could walk down steps, cross the dirt road, and stand alongside a river. I could feel and hear the breeze move through the branches of the poplar trees on the river's bank. It was all familiar. All known to me. It was real.

I didn't share these memories with anyone at that time, but in July of 1995, I had an experience that allowed me to acknowledge that these vivid recollections were ones I wanted to claim as my own and experience in more detail. My sister, Kathleen, and her husband, Doug, had been visiting for the wedding of one of our five daughters. The day after the wedding, my husband Terry, Kathleen, Doug, and I took a day trip to Victoria, British Columbia. It was a warm, sunny summer's day, and we strolled through the side streets, examining the wares of vendors and artisans, commenting again and again on how wonderful the wedding had been and how great it was to be together in Victoria.

As we slowly walked along, my eyes caught those of a young woman in her vendor tent, which was labeled "Palm Readings." We smiled at one another and I continued walking with my family. After five minutes or so, I turned to Terry and told him I had to go back and see her. This was a very unusual thing for me to do, as I had never had my palm read nor had any interest in doing so. However, the pull toward this person was so strong that I handed my husband my jewelry and bag and headed back to her.

The woman's tent was approximately five feet by five feet, tiny really. Two chairs faced each other and off to the side was a small table on which sat some printed material and two round balls of crystal, each the size of a large orange. One was pale pink and the other clear with flecks of white and silver-gray. She motioned for me to sit in one of the folding chairs and asked me to hold the clear ball in both hands. She pulled her chair to the small table, never glancing toward me. After a few minutes, she asked if I felt anything. I told her I felt nothing. She got up from her chair and brought the pink ball with her and handed it to me as she took the clear one. She wasn't back in her chair more than thirty seconds when I told her I was feeling something. The crystal ball was becoming warm in my hands. Very warm. The feeling was both unexpected and disconcerting.

She got up, removed the ball from my hands, placed it on the table, pulled her chair across from mine, and told me she would now read both my palms. In one, she said, she saw the past and in the other the present and future.

She proceeded to tell me specific details about my life over the previous twenty years. I said little, wanting to neither confirm nor deny anything she said, lest I give any hint leading her to think what she was telling me was false or true. What she told me of my life was indeed true; the accuracy of her knowledge was quite astonishing. To think a stranger could know these aspects of my past! But that was only the beginning of my surprise.

When she lifted my other palm and began to talk of the present and of my future, her words came fast. I wanted to remember everything she said and had a hard time keeping up with her. She told me I was in a "healing profession" and worked primarily with children. She said I was a teacher and therapist, all of which was and is true. She asked if I ever thought about the fact that my work resulted in helping others in ways that were sometimes not easily explained. At this point I told her yes, that I felt I often connected with patients, particularly children, on a deep, intuitive level that could not always be explained scientifically or in the context of my training and experience as a speech-language pathologist.

She told me that to my present life I brought experiences and training from a past life. She said I was very intuitive and those I taught and worked with knew I cared deeply for them, and because of that, they were able to respond openly and with trust.

She then asked if I had knowledge or memories of any past lives. My heart began to race. I was at odds as to how to answer this question. Tears came to my eyes as I realized that the vivid dreams I had been having were of patients that I had cared for in a very real place in another time. She could see I had at least three past lives. I shared with her that the majority of my memories of a previous time were during and after World War I, in France.

I left that palm reader feeling shaken to my core. I was also extremely excited, and as I rejoined my family, my only thought was to find a place to sit and write down everything she had told me and to begin to write my memories as well. On the ferry trip back to the United States, I made hasty notes of all I remembered and typed it up when we returned home.

After our trip, however, the responsibilities of a busy mother and wife as well as working full-time in my career as a speech-language pathologist were paramount, and I wasn't able to attend to and truly focus on what kept knocking persistently in my mind, asking me to pay attention and remember. In 2010, I began to write down everything I remembered. The story didn't come to me in a sequential order; the middle chapters of this book came first, followed by the beginning and ending chapters. I wrote them each in whatever order they were recalled, and amazingly, they have flowed into a story of a life I remember living. I have spent the last two years expanding my memories into this narrative, doing a great deal of research along the way, verifying the historical accuracy of what happened in France during those years surrounding WWI, and staying true to the memories of Marie Durant Chagall and our shared experiences.

This journey of remembering with Marie has been unique and life changing, and I hope you enjoy it as well.

CHAPTER 1

GROWING UP IN MARSEILLE, 1905 – 1915

The swirling, gusting wind thrust Solange and me forward in bursts and fits. I secured my large purple hood under my chin with my right hand; my left was gripped by my sister. We had been marketing at the shops and stalls along the waterfront when an early spring mistral caught us completely unawares. As we ran, our market bags flew out sideways and slapped themselves back against our chilled bodies whenever they caught spurts of air. My ankle-high boots were filling with water from above and below as the darkening sky dropped hail-filled rain, which pelted our faces and lay heavy on our woolen capes and hoods. Again and again, the blinding white swords in the sky were accompanied by great *boom*s of sound.

"Solange, Solange! Look!" I called over the wild howling of the wind, pointing to the dock.

The ships bobbed in the turbulence and swayed side to side while sailors, also surprised by this sudden storm, frantically rushed to secure their decks. To my eight-year-old eyes, those men resembled no more than tiny sailors on little toy ships I sometimes saw boys playing with (and secretly coveted for myself). I wondered which ones were Papa's ships and Papa's sailors. I stopped and stared with a great desire to leap aboard and become a toy sailor myself. I could work on Papa's ships and be with him always on his travels.

Solange tugged my arm, shouting, "Marie, hurry! Stop your dawdling and stay up with me. We are soaked to the bone!"

We ran along the waterfront for another few minutes before turning north onto our own *rue*, toward home. Ours was a rowhouse constructed of burnt-red brick. All of the houses looked very similar, save for their detailing, and the front doors were positioned on the left side of each home. Two stories high with tall, wide windows front and back, the house was broad and square, solid and safe. Before opening the front door and stepping from the street into the foyer, Solange had us shake ourselves several times, sending the wet flying off our cloaks. Once inside, she swept away our capes to the kitchen to dry them on hooks by the stove.

The thick carpet just inside the front door, in tones of deep red, blues, and yellows and handwoven in India according to Solange, was splotched with water from our entrance but still drier by far than most of myself. I sat down on the rug, untied my laces, and released my feet from the wet leather. Scooting on my bottom to find a new dry spot, I leaned back against the wall beside the door and looked about our house.

The walls of the ground floor were paneled with dark, luminous oak that forever smelled of wax and lemon polish. Those smells, mingled with the lingering scent of Papa's pipe tobacco, were to me the smells of home. The high ceilings were decorated round the tops of the walls with contrasting woods carved with scrollwork and intricate designs. My eyes moved along the familiar shapes, identifying what I thought to be pinecones, leaves, and perhaps a cluster of grapes here and there.

The foyer, which extended almost five meters to the right and three meters in front of me, gleamed in square marble tiles of black and gray stone specked with red and silver. To the right, a wide opening led into the sitting room, with the dining area to its right. Papa's office, his place of meeting and business when he was home, was located opposite the sitting room. Throughout the living areas, the waxed oak floors were covered with richly colored wool carpets from around the world. I stood up and walked into the sitting room, where a welcoming fire blazed in the carved stone hearth at the center of the room. This was the focal point and place of gathering in our home and where I curled up in front of the fire to warm up. Tapestried divans and armchairs with ottomans sat semi-circled round the hearth, accompanied by a low rectangular cherry wood coffee table set with cups for tea. Smaller side tables, chairs, and a settee made up another seating area. This is where Solange and I spent much of our time reading, doing our needlework and stitching, and taking lessons from our tutors.

To the right of the sitting room was the expansive dining room, with our dark carved mahogany table already set for twelve for that evening's dinner. The spacious kitchen, a substantial pantry, and several smaller rooms were located on the other side of the hearth wall. Our cook and housekeeper Elise's bedroom was there, as was a small storeroom she used for laundry and housekeeping supplies. A catchall area, long and narrow, was at the rear of the house, with a back door that led into a small garden where Elise tended her herbs and vegetables. We sat there often in the summer evenings, attempting to catch a breeze from the sea before retiring to the tight, close heat of the upstairs bedrooms. More than once, Solange and I found ourselves on such nights half-asleep, lying on a blanket, identifying the constellations Papa so loved and wondering if he was doing the same wherever he might be. Four bedrooms were on the second floor, and although Solange and I had separate rooms, we always slept together in hers. Back then, I often thought Papa, when home, must have slept in his office, as his bed seldom appeared ruffled.

Solange was six years older than me, and though we shared a common paternity, our features must surely have resembled our own mothers', for Solange was as dark as I was fair. Dark and light; patient and impatient; reddish-brown- and blue-eyed; tall and taller. Solange and Marie. Solange had spent some time with both our mothers and told me she had loved them both well. I glimpsed but one, only briefly and unremembered—my own dear *maman*. She left us, passing in the night as I turned six days and Solange turned six years.

As we grew older, though as sisters we were opposites in so many ways, our voices claimed us as kin. Our contralto voices, deeper than typical for women, held the same rich timbre and were never more lovely than when Solange sang harmony to my melody. Try as I might, I could never accustom my ear to create Solange's beautiful harmonies, so that was left to her. We loved to sing, and Papa would often teach us snippets of songs he picked up from foreign ports of call. He never seemed to remember all the words, though, and it was obvious whenever he began to make them up. When we pressed him to tell us "the real words," he would laugh and explain that many of the songs were passed from sailor to sailor, and not all were fit for the ears of young ladies. We would merely improvise new words, singing heartily and with gusto. At the endings of such a time of song, we three would sit very still with lingering smiles and tears of laughter in our eyes. Papa would slap both hands on his thighs and declare that nothing prepared a being for eating supper like a good round of singing.

Our love of music swirled round us as we sang and hummed through our days, doing our fine stitching, cooking, and walking to and from and about town. Solange would inevitably find a tune suitable for any event and most particularly for the townspeople we might cross paths with, as many were indeed our familiar acquaintances. She sang her opinions and comments rather than stating them in mere words. For Father Xavier and a party of mourners solemnly making their way to the cemetery: a snippet of a dirge. For Monsieur Cambrey stumbling across the stones and smelling of drink as he passed: a snatch of one of Papa's sailor songs. For a mother with a carefully tucked babe in arms: a Brahms lullaby. And for Madame Dubrey, loudly scolding while tugging on the ears of her raucous twin boys: a bit of quick Mozart. Solange was at her most playful and witty during these times of musical observation, always acknowledged by me with a laugh, sigh, or some sound that we both understood. Music infused our lives, illuminating even the most recurring and familiar events with a meaning particular to shared moments. We would hum Debussy while Elise lifted hot bread from the oven just before we eagerly pulled off crusty bites and filled our mouths while butter dripped down our lips. Only Debussy's eloquence could describe the indescribable.

During our very young years after my maman passed, Papa attempted to install a series of "highly experienced" nannies, cooks, and housekeepers.

Solange, always a fierce and feisty youngster, approached each new caretaker as a threat and challenge to be conquered and tossed from our door. Solange of Exceptional Fortitude (Papa's nom de plume for her whenever she pontificated a newly devised plan of action against the current caregiver) connived ever more intolerable antics to convince each new nanny that they were never, ever going to replace our *mamans* and that the only place they needed to fill was the doorway as they left our lives.

After a rather hasty exit by the fourth nanny within a year, Solange explained to Papa very formally, an attitude she carried off well, that neither she (nine at the time) nor I needed any nanny whatsoever. She was completely capable of taking care of the both of us. We needed only a good cook and full-time housekeeper because the present ones were inferior, she informed Papa. She also wanted to discuss tutors and, of course, had a plan as to beginning our schooling. Papa had always told us that when the time came for learning, our school would be at home. That suited Solange, and what suited her suited me as well. Years later, amidst laughter, Solange and Papa both agreed that the one nanny who had outlasted the other three by at least two months seemed to have had a high tolerance for ear-piercing screams, bites that scarred, and kicks resulting in shin bruises. Solange of Exceptional Fortitude indeed!

She and I loved each other fiercely, and togetherness was our constant. Papa, now at his wit's end trying to run home and business and provide for these two young children, looked from one to the other of his small, daring daughters. Solange had made this bold proposal after breakfast one morning, for which we had appeared especially well groomed in fine dresses with our hair in braids, as Papa preferred. Holding hands, postures straight, and looking up at Papa with expressions exuding confidence, we presented a strong case, and Papa relented to all of Solange's demands. He agreed to a six-month trial without a nanny and to the other staff being replaced as soon as possible. Solange insisted she be present during the interviews for the cook and housekeeper, and together she and Papa would make the final decision. And then they would begin looking for tutors as well.

Did Papa then smile at this bold, pragmatically feisty elder daughter of his? Did he see the faithfully committed, future aide-de-camp she was to become to him?

Solange and Papa were much alike. Indeed, he must have seen in her the same solid determination to hold our small family tightly together by relying on our own strengths and unity. Although I knew only that she had, with great seriousness, instructed me to stand beside her, still and quiet, and to look only at Papa as she spoke to him of her plan, I understood, as young as I was, that Solange had secured a victory for us that day and that we could now look forward to peace in our home.

Over the next two weeks, Solange and Papa interviewed a series of cooks and housekeepers. At the end of the final afternoon of applicants filing to and from our home, we all sat together as Papa and Solange decided who would become a part of our household. "I want women with kind eyes and ready smiles. That is important, for are we not to be a family, Papa?" said Solange.

It was agreed upon that a capable woman named Elise would become both our cook and housekeeper. And so Solange, at this young age of nine, began her career as domestic arbiter, creating in our home a warm and comfortable atmosphere for the three of us. From her flowed a gift for employing and supporting all those who became part of our day-to-day experiences. She wove all of us together—cook and housekeeper, tutors, and friends—tapping into each person's natural abilities to create a home that was full of wonderful smells, much laughter, engaging conversation, intellectual pursuits, and a papa who was secure and content in the knowledge that his own dear daughters were happy and thriving.

Papa screened each of the tutors carefully, surely based on recommendations from his own circle of friends and acquaintances, and Solange's teachers became mine. They were always men—some young and some very old, some stuffy and others whimsical. Some smelled rather like mothballs, tobacco, or old socks. Some had wit and kind demeanors. Papa and Solange chose our teachers judged not only by their education and knowledge in their particular areas of expertise but also by whether they would be good matches for what Papa called "our home education."

Math, music, philosophy, languages, and the arts were all exciting subjects of study, but my favorite was history. History not only of past world events but also the way in which people had lived throughout time—how they thought about their world and each other. Religion also held a fascination for me, as we practiced none ourselves. Most of our acquaintances were Catholic or Jewish, and I looked with great curiosity and longing as we passed churches and synagogues when walking to and from town. The study of history often intersected into the world of religion, and I was an enthusiastic student of both.

As Papa traveled often and extensively, he had our teachers provide him with lists of which books, maps, or other items they might require to augment our studies. Crates of books and such would arrive every few months, and opening and unpacking all that Papa sent home from so many faraway places became for us our holidays. We spent long hours inspecting our academic gifts as well as beautiful jewelry, artifacts, and unexpected treasures. We knew even then, and spoke of it often as we grew older, that our education was exceptional and that Papa was our greatest teacher and advocate. We knew he despaired of leaving us so frequently at home for such long periods of time and that the delivery of exotic items from faraway places somewhat assuaged his guilt. We did indeed appreciate those tokens of his love.

Papa chose well, and over the years our home acquired small works of art, which sat on tables and hung on walls, sprinkled judiciously around our home. He was endlessly delighted to find them about when he returned from his travels and would tell us the story surrounding each acquisition. It was exciting and grand, as each book and treasure always seemed surrounded by adventure. Papa's constant good nature and affection toward Solange and me were his greatest gifts though. To these we held fast and returned toward him one hundredfold.

Papa was a self-made man, widely read and more widely traveled. His places of study were the ports of Europe and the peoples of differing cultures he experienced while conducting his business. On his returns home, in the rare quiet evenings we spent alone with him, we pried from him new and exhilarating stories. He spoke several languages, but because he could not write them as well as speak them, he insisted that Solange and I be equally proficient in written and spoken Italian and English as in our native French. To this end, two days each week, we would speak only in a particular language. Italian was my favorite; I often dreamed of visiting Italia. With Elise, we carefully prepared "language meals" for those days and all ate together, teaching Elise phrases in Italian or English.

Papa also insisted we become "accomplished in domestic skills." Elise had practiced since childhood the arts of needlework, embroidery, and sewing and along with cooking taught us these as well. She became a great friend and *confidente*, and we passed endless hours in the kitchen kneading and baking while she told us tales of her life growing up the oldest of twelve siblings. She began cooking as she took her first steps, she was fond of saying. When Papa was gone, we passed most winter evenings with her, making meals in the kitchen and afterward working on needlework, chatting late into the night. An endless source of hugs and witticisms, Elise was warm and loving and our great matron.

With time, Solange began to assume more of the responsibilities of running the house, expanding and managing her domestic chores with ease and enjoyment. Though she was efficient to the extreme in ensuring the house was well organized and operating smoothly, she was ever calm and able to focus her intensity inward. My intensity, on the other hand, was all focused outward.

Solange had a keen sense of propriety, always aware that we were extensions of others' perceptions of Papa. She constantly reminded me that our behavior and demeanor were closely observed in the markets of town, assessed at our ladies' gatherings and volunteer events, and scrutinized by all who passed through our home. We were never more studied than when Papa hosted dinners with business associates round our dining table.

As young as twelve, and together with Elise, Solange began to orchestrate Papa's business dinners and soirees. Solange and Papa would discuss whom to invite, the seating arrangements, and what would be prepared and served, including the wine to accompany each course. She demonstrated such astute insights, both culinary and social, as well as an innate political savviness, that after the first year of mutual planning, Papa merely told her the date and guest list and she planned and executed, with ingenuity and grace, each dinner thereafter. Wines that were served were usually grown by someone in attendance, while another's caviar and olives were at the table, and still another's *truffles au chocolat*. Everyone felt welcomed, and Solange and I were always aware of the great sense of regard toward Papa as he bestowed upon each guest respect and acknowledgement. It was business, but refined business, with the expectation that during dinner all would be conducted with decorum and good grace.

By the age of sixteen, Solange easily engaged in conversation with these men of commerce. Papa's associates came to relish an invitation to our home, knowing the business would be carried out around excellent food and charming conversation. Solange sat at one end of the table and Papa at the other. I occasionally saw one of these businessmen cast an interested eye upon Solange in a way that had nothing to do with talk of shipping and commerce, and noticed that Papa saw it as well, though Solange never seemed to, or chose not to. In our years in Marseille, I never knew Solange to show more than a polite interest in any of the men, young or old, who graced our table and our home.

I was always present as well and sat at Papa's right. His pride in his daughters was apparent. Being younger and at times not totally at ease, I rarely engaged in the conversation. But ever considerate, Papa at some point in every dinner would place his hand round my back and comment on my latest accomplishment in music or art—something to acknowledge and include me in the evening's conversation. I would squirm and fidget, eventually becoming bored by the conversation, but always I felt included and, taking cues from Solange, attempted to present my most ladylike self.

At the end of the several-course meal served and cleared by lady friends of Elise, the men retired to father's office to "get the business settled." They would rise as one and move to the other side of the house into Papa's large study. There they would be provided cigars or tobacco for their pipes, and Solange would offer brandy poured in cut crystal glasses from the cart waiting just inside Papa's study door. She and I would then go up to our rooms and go over every detail of that night's event. After an hour or so, we would begin to hear cordial goodbyes and knew Papa would have concluded all the arrangements for his next round of shipments. After the last gentlemen left, we would call down our good-nights to Papa and he would return them to us.

Papa's business grew thanks as much to Solange's good efforts as to the boom in trade brought on by a country standing in ready preparation at the edges of a coming conflict. During those years, Papa frequently accompanied one of his ships to some foreign port. He was a man of action and hated being "cooped up on land." He said he felt "vital on the sea," and I envied him this freedom to come and go. And so he would leave us for two weeks or more, usually within a few days after one of the dinners. Solange and I would feel a sense of freedom as just she, Elise, and I filled our days as we chose.

When Papa was gone, we also explored the ever-expanding town, attending concerts and readings. There was always the required presence of "other genteel ladies," as Papa described them, to accompany us to all social gatherings and events. We would reciprocate and invite friends into our home for tea or lunch, which most often included a reading or music performance by an artist either local or passing through Marseille. I am sure that Solange paid them well, and these, our own soirees, were much enjoyed by all and, as Solange ever said, "increased Papa's esteem."

And thus, many years flowed along. Solange, always constant, appeared happy and content. But as the years passed and the town around me became familiar in the extreme, the world and its unfolding events beckoned me to stretch beyond our predictable life. I became more and more restless.

Solange recognized the signs of my malcontent and made concerted efforts to keep me busy and engaged. She added tutors and teachers, and when I was approaching sixteen, she employed a dance instructor. She even planned two small dance socials during that year for when Papa was home. The furniture from our dining room was removed to create a ballroom, and our house was filled with music and friends. I knew her intentions and understood both her and Papa's motives for wanting to keep me settled, but these activities in no way calmed my disquiet.

During this period, Solange also required me to complete a list of dinner-party responsibilities that she insisted she did not have time for herself. I did them halfheartedly and not altogether well. Those tasks to engage me were the result of my pulling away and her compensating attempt to bring me back close. I continued to push back her encouragements to become more involved in the planning and arranging of Papa's formal business dinners. Still, she prompted me to put forth ideas and plans for excursions and activities that I might especially enjoy. I truly felt there was little left in Marseille that could prove interesting or fulfill the sense of increasing longing to move, and move beyond this place so secure and predictable.

I did not want to become an extension of my beloved sister. She found meaning and purpose in the life she had successfully created. She exuded a peaceful satisfaction with an existence I was beginning to find suffocating. Solange's life was well suited to her talents, and I was ripping myself at my seams, eager to create one that suited me half as well. Like Papa, I had an intense need to feel "vital"—to move, explore, and find myself caught up in places I knew nothing of but wanted to experience nonetheless. My desire to expand outside and beyond my physical and emotional self caused sharp corners in my moods, and more than once I cut Solange with my biting tongue.

Perhaps my state of mind was more than youthful restlessness. Perhaps I reflected as well the uncertainty and changing of those times. The talk of political turmoil and conflict made the edges of the days feel singed with worried anticipation. The climate all around us was restless, and while people held fast to their predictable flow of months and years, the tides of change were approaching, and I was poised to ride its current.

CHAPTER 2

PAPA, 1913 – 1915

Papa was a barrel of a man, round and broad-chested, set on thin legs. Always overheated, he wore as few layers of clothing as possible while still maintaining the dress of a gentleman of business. An exterior resembling either a roaring blaze of booming energy or the carefully tended embers of dampened flames mirrored the heat within him. His thick chestnut hair rolled in waves across his head and extended his height to almost two meters. In the sun, russet tones highlighted those waves but especially his sideburns, mustache, and beard. Tinges of gray appeared gradually, and the bulk of him seemed to diminish during that time before war as his business intensified and the tensions of impending conflict were common dinnertime conversations.

I did not want to think the graying of my papa had anything to do with advancing age or worry, but I saw during that period how his red-brown eyes, so like Solange's, reflected the strain brought on by overwork and stress. He was our rock—our world, really—and though wearied with fatigue, he was always willing to tell us stories and anecdotes of his travels with good humor. His adventures were our gateway into a broader, more exciting world.

Papa would crackle and sparkle as he held court with his business comrades at our dinner fêtes, peppering the conversations with political opinions cloaked in sarcastic, wry wit. With the exit of each dinner guest, he wound down a little more until it was just the three of us, and he would once again become just our papa. He was worldly, educated, and wise, yet rooted deeply in all things practical. Commerce was his passion, his daughters and home his sanctuary to protect, and politics his religion.

When talk turned to shipping and trade routes, ships and cargo, his eyes would shine as dark jewels. With hands waving, his thoughts flowed so quickly that words tumbled over themselves, and not until his face was red did he remember to take a breath. "Innovation" was his message, and he was an impassioned messenger for changing the "old ways of commerce." "Forward, forward!" was his motto regarding his business, our education, the state of the world, everything.

Solange always filled in the blanks of life while attempting to answer my constant barrage of questions. What was it exactly Papa did in his business? Which were his ships? Where did they go? What did they carry?

When I was about twelve and began to ask these questions more frequently, Solange took me down to the harbor to show me Papa's fleet of ships. He had converted sailing vessels to steamers, and these ships moved goods to and from ports up and down the coastline of France and, more often now, as far north as Spain.

On our frequent trips to the markets, I would more likely than not try to engage Solange in conversation related to my desire to go exploring with Papa.

"Look, Solange," I said, pointing to a ship pulling out of the harbor. "Do you not think that must be one of Papa's? I do think we are old enough to join him on an adventure soon. That would be so wonderful!"

"While it may sound very exciting, Marie, Papa wants us to keep our feet firmly planted on the ground and leave the sea to him," she replied flatly.

Moving down the rows of vessels, I asked, as I had multiple times, "Do you not think we could ask him just to take us aboard and show us where he sleeps?" I persisted. "I would gladly ask him when we get home."

"You may ask, dear sister, as we both have at least two dozen times before, but until Papa is ready and willing, we will most likely not be walking the deck of a ship, much less exploring its underbelly. Patience, Marie. Papa has promised that one day we will travel together to wherever we might want to go. I can hardly believe that might really happen, but you know Papa is a man of his word."

And so our lives proceeded, growing up in Marseille ruled by routine and constancy. Papa built his business, Solange and I focused on our education and social pastimes, and when Papa was in port, our otherwise quiet home was filled with dinners and guests.

As time moved forward, the talk of politics and the possibility of armed conflict became more frequent. The topic of war now fueled the fires of conversation well beyond our polite dinner banter with Papa's guests. Papa would either be the most intensely loud or contribute the least to the verbose conversations regarding Germany and impending war. I often kept count of the number of glasses of wine each dinner guest had drunk to determine whether there was a correlation between wine consumption and a guest's escalating emotional outbursts that sometimes bordered on rage. At that point, Papa invariably would excuse Solange and me from the table, and we would slide up the stairs toward our rooms only to sit on the landing and eavesdrop on conversations we did not understand. Eventually, such talk instilled a deep sense of fear in both of us. When we became too tired or too frightened, or both, we would climb into Solange's bed and huddle together until sleep came. Come the new day, Papa never referenced discussions at the table from the night before.

We began to see reflected in Papa's eyes his heightened sense of anxiety and his own fear as well as ours. We were all anxious in those days. Everyone everywhere we went whispered the rumors of war and what it might mean. One woman friend paid us a call during a rare afternoon when Papa was at home. She began to expound over tea that it was "God's truth" that war was "pulling at our bonnet strings" and that we needed to "be prepared or we will lose our heads as well as our hats!" Papa swiftly thanked her for calling upon us and escorted her to the door.

Papa would often try and calm those who expressed agitation and fear. We all knew that the worry was based on more than rumors now. It was 1913, and fighting had begun, but we did not know if or when it would come close to us. The fire within him burned quietly in those days of unrest and worried anticipation but never more than when someone would comment about "this Jew" or "that Jew" who was thinking of closing his tailoring business or his dry goods store.

Papa's eyes would burn and his jaw would stiffen but he made no comment. The men referred to were well respected and successful and counted among Papa's many friends. Solange, who handled all the details of Papa's business, told me of two such businessmen thinking of closing and leaving France. They were also Papa's prime source for monetary transactions, she said. I did not truly understand that significance but knew only that it frightened me even more to think of friends contemplating the need to leave our country. Why, and where would they go? Nothing made sense. Papa became quiet and absorbed, and the gray began to further invade his russet waves.

As 1914 approached, he also became more absent from home. His time was consumed by the increasing demands on shipping that readiness for war required. There were no more dinner parties and fewer social events. When Solange and I did go out, it was to market or to volunteer at church or Red Cross functions. When Papa was at home, men would come to see him alone or in pairs, meeting with him only behind the closed door of his study. Solange kept a cart in there readied with brandy, clean glasses, and a plate of savories. The glasses almost always gave evidence of having been used, but the food was seldom touched. After a while, Solange simplified the tray's contents to include only clean glasses, drink, and tobacco.

Only in those rare times at home now, with just the three of us, would Papa's eyes soften and his voice become gentle as he shared with us his concerns. He would speak slowly, his voice pitched lower. It was as though each articulated sentence necessitated a singular focus to form speech from thoughts. We knew we could ask him anything and he would provide us with an answer he felt was honest and wise. We always felt safe, loved, and worthy.

I was ever curious regarding our lack of religious practice and what it was exactly that Papa did believe. Most of our social acquaintances were Catholic and always going to Mass on this or that holy day. Why did we not attend services of any kind? It was the topic I most dearly wanted to discuss with him. The many times I attempted to broach the subject directly, however, he would only talk of religion from the perspective of our education and world history. But, I would argue, everyone had a religion; everyone came from some particular culture, and I wanted to know more about ours. Early on in my inquiries Solange told me Papa and her mother were both Jewish, but she did not know if my Belgian-born mother was as well. It wasn't until much later in life that I came to understand the weight of Papa's concerns, the significance of his wanting us to understand our heritage but by remaining vague and allusive feeling he was protecting us from possible future repercussions.

At those times when Papa waxed eloquent after two glasses of brandy, only then did I feel I could venture into questions of faith. One such evening with a few minutes alone with Papa, I dared ask, "Papa, if we are Jewish, why do we not go to synagogue or observe Sabbath and holy days? I feel like we are hiding our history. Are we ashamed of our faith, or do you not believe in any religion at all?"

Sitting me down beside him with a serious intensity I had seldom seen in him, he told me, "Religion and heritage is a mantle placed on your wet head at birth. It is with you when you come in and will be with you when you leave."

"But Papa, our faith is rich in history and rituals. Why can we not celebrate who we are? It is confusing, and I do wish you would give a concrete answer!" I cried, my voice increasing in volume.

Papa replied with patience in his eyes. "Marie, we do not need to perform rituals to know who we are, or for anyone with eyes to know who we are not. A wise man observes the rituals of others and keeps his own to himself."

Again I pushed. "I find it frustrating and certainly would like to at least enjoy a Sabbath with my papa and sister. Is that really too much to ask?"

"Yes, Marie, it is! It is also unwise to even consider doing so. I know too well your frustration, as I felt much the same when I was younger. My parents also told me to hold my countenance." He paused and took my hand, gripping it tightly in both of his. "Explore your heritage within the confines of history. Study the ancient teachings of all religions, and then hold yours in your heart as your own. We do not have to discuss this again, *ma chère*. I ask only that you trust what I tell you."

As thankful as I was for Papa's words, my questions still lacked sufficient answers. When I shared this conversation with Solange, she told me she had in the past asked Papa if we might celebrate Jewish customs, and he had told her the same—adding that our home was visited by many but to be known by few. He forbade what he called "relics of faith" of any kind in the house.

We once asked if we could have a rabbi tutor us in Judaic history and religion. He forbade that as well, saying Judaism was only to be studied in the context of history and world religions and that our history tutor was certainly adequate to cover them all. Papa did sometimes quiz us regarding our understanding of various religions—Christianity, Buddhism, and Islam, always ending with questions about Judaism. He discussed with us the historical, social, and economic influence of each, how world conflicts were rooted in religious ideology, and how religions shaped the lands and peoples who embraced their faiths.

"And with Judaism," I asked, "was there a country where it was the one religion practiced?"

Looking from Solange to myself, he said, "Jews do not have a country but are a living mystery lived by its people in countries all over the world. Forty days was only the beginning, as we have been strewn across the world and are wandering still."

Solange and I had not heard him speak so personally of this mysterious faith of ours before. We held ourselves perfectly still and silent and, in doing so, hoped that he might continue to share his thoughts.

And then with a smile he added, "If we are God's chosen, He has a precarious way for us to live."

"But Papa, France is our home and our country!" I responded.

"Yes, child. France is our country but not our land. And we will not always be such free tenants."

I could not have known then how very wise Papa was.

CHAPTER 3

NURSING,
JULY 1915 – APRIL 1916

Three times a week, Solange and I walked to the Catholic church close to the wharf. With each passing week, the French Red Cross attempted to crowd together more tables and chairs to provide the growing numbers of volunteers a place to either sit or stand to cut, roll, and stuff the empty boxes full of bandages to send off to the field hospitals.

The chatter was constant and caused me great agitation. The party atmosphere among the ladies seemingly dressed for tea felt disrespectful. Solange told me to put my "nose down," that my "sensibilities" were showing. Now seventeen years old, I had quite a well-developed sense of self-righteousness.

I had dressed in my house clothes, adding only a plain muslin apron over my house frock. I was serious about this work and felt my simple mode of dress appropriate for such. Solange was dressed down as well, and more because of the wind than decorum, we wore no hats, instead winding our hair in tight chignons to the back of our necks. I admit to a few silent giggles while watching the ladies as they struggled to hold on to their hats while one-handedly rolling gauze with its flying white tail. Not an easy business, but for them, a hat on one's head was at least as important as bandages in the box!

Though committed to the work, these thrice-weekly sessions added to my sense of frustration and restlessness. I wanted to bolt and run as soon as we would find a place at a table and begin the endless hours with gauze. Solange was a master of polite conversation and would occasionally place a gentle hand on my knee, as though calming a restless colt and, I knew, to encourage me to contribute an appropriate comment now and again. What would I do without her? She truly was my touchstone, keeping me focused and steady while I attempted to find some meaning to it all.

The parish priest always hovered about, moving table to table, exclaiming what great work was being accomplished in God's name. Today was no different. Red-faced and looking damp, with a wheeze to his breathing, he was even more talkative than his usual blustering self.

The Red Cross officially organized these volunteer efforts; the church's property was merely a convenient locale to meet. The priest, however, apparently assumed that any activity on his sacred ground constituted the work of his church. He voiced great pride in doing his part for "our brave soldiers." Not for the first time, I wondered what was involved in his "doing his part," as I never once saw him roll a bandage or pack a box.

Through chats with our fellow volunteers, we learned that the Red Cross was asking for the use of vacant buildings or spaces, even homes, that could be set up as hospitals closer to the fighting up north yet some distance west of the front. Our group of volunteers had also discussed converting a vacant building in town where local returning wounded could be cared for and hopefully rehabilitated.

On this particular day, at the end of our second hour of work, the priest moved to the front of the tent and, shouting over the sudden bursts of wind, with great intensity introduced to us a Red Cross nurse. The sudden appearance of a Red Cross nurse certainly caught our attention, and we stopped our work to listen. She told us that later in the week a doctor would come to speak about training volunteer nurses to fill the increasing need.

Now I knew the cause for the priest's overexcitement. I am sure he felt personally responsible for the Red Cross representative's upcoming visit. Again, it seemed, he was adding another notch to his growing godliness. I was certainly in a mood that day. However, my ears perked up at the words "training volunteer nurses"!

The nurse, a tall, middle-aged woman with a weary but commanding presence, went on to ask us to "spread the news" regarding the meeting and to invite those who might be interested or have monies to donate to help with this effort of finding and training nurses. Someone asked if men could apply; the answer was that it was a good use of a man's time if he wasn't actively serving. We all knew men who felt discouraged because they had not been accepted into the military. She said strong backs were needed as well as gentle hands. I would think a tolerance for blood and bewilderment was necessary as well. I could do this. Nothing bothered my "sensibilities"!

I heard myself asking the nurse how long the meeting would be. Was it going to be held here on the lawn or inside the church? Did she have any more specifics regarding what the training entailed? Was the training weeks or months? Where was the training held? Where would trainees be sent? After listening to my litany of questions, the nurse responded only that the meeting would begin at 10:00 a.m. or "whenever the doctor arrived thereafter" and that it would last no more than an hour and be held in the meeting room in the basement of the church.

The priest was also pressed for information but reiterated only what the nurse had already explained. They knew nothing more, but I wanted to know everything more. The nurse departed—on to the next town to continue her recruiting efforts. We could only wait for our meeting and hope the doctor could provide answers to all questions.

The priest asked if any of us would be attending the meeting with the doctor, if we might see ourselves as nurses. There were very few among our group who were still unmarried or not attached in some way to jobs or other responsibilities. Many of the women had already taken positions in the canneries, the local foundry, or metalworking factories. Their men had gone to the North, and the women were attempting to keep their families together, juggling caring for their children and working long hours at jobs suddenly made vacant by the town's lack of manpower. The conversation turned to worry about the children coming home to empty houses and how thankful the mothers were for older women as well as those with older children willing to care for younger ones while their mothers worked.

It seemed everyone but Solange and me was engaged in working outside the home or helping tend other women's children. In reality, Solange, with Papa, was engaged in work never-ending and never more so than with the increasing trade generated by the war machine. Solange increasingly spent her time completing documents, arranging shipment upon shipment as countries prepared for war. The massive amounts of paperwork were daunting, and she worked long into the night, staying up late with Papa whenever he was home. He was now busy with overland shipments as well as those by sea. She had shared with me that she sometimes suspected many of Papa's services to France and the Allies were clandestine, as he asked her not to inquire about what was being sent or the destination. These shipments went without official manifests. Her constant support of Papa in these endeavors, the ongoing challenge of keeping him well fed, and the less-than-adequate sleep for them both left her busier than ever and worried about it all. She became quieter and more reserved. Her liveliness receded as the work became more stressful and her resources flagged.

And there I was, unsettled and without purpose, seeking an experience to both satisfy myself and to provide assistance to others. Coupled with that, I felt a recurring sense of guilt. I was doing nothing more than rolling these white strips of cloth. I could do more. Something worthy, selfless, and so exhausting that I would sleep soundly at night.

And so that day, when the nurse told us about the upcoming meeting, as we finished up our work, Solange attempted to catch my eye. I quickly looked away but not fast enough to miss the set of her jaw and her hands moving too quickly to roll the last of the gauze even more tightly. I knew her mind as well as she knew mine. She knew I would go to hear the doctor speak. We were indeed going to have an interesting conversation on the way home, but while I had made up my mind, I would appease her by stating I was merely interested in knowing what was involved, that I had no actual intentions of volunteering to be a nurse. I would assure her I would only listen and obtain information. But I knew she would not believe me, just as I did not believe it myself.

Before we made it to the street, she quickly turned to me, her voice in hushed but urgent tones, "Marie, you cannot, *cannot* even play with the idea of becoming a nurse! It is dangerous, and Papa would never, ever relent to such a request!"

"Play? You think I would be playing by considering this opportunity to do something useful? I would hope you would hold my abilities to make rational considerations and decisions in higher regard, dear sister! I could do this, you know!"

"It isn't a matter of whether you could or could not become a nurse. Of course you could! But the question is why would you? There is much you can do here without sacrificing your safety or well-being off in some dangerous place far from home. Papa will forbid it. You know that, don't you?"

I stopped in the street and placed my hand on her arm. "Solange, please look beyond your worries for me and Papa's concerns. Surely you know I have not been altogether happy or at peace for some time now. Please tell me you understand. You know me better than anyone. Would you hold me back from attempting to find what it is I desire to do? Prevent me from becoming more than I am here? Tell me you understand and will help me!"

Before we turned to the front entrance of home, we had reached a compromise that I would go to the meeting and listen to the information the recruiting doctor provided. I would commit to nothing before talking with Solange further. She begged to go with me, but I did not want to be distracted by the thoughts floating from her mind to mine. I wanted to be free to consider what might be.

And so I went alone and found twelve women already seated in the basement of the church's meeting room. Among them were those I did not know and women I knew by brief acquaintance from town but none within our close social circle. There were none from our bandaging and boxing contingent. I silently harrumphed, thinking of course they would not be here, but word had obviously spread of the meeting, and I wondered what the intentions were of these other women.

I discerned from scattered conversations that some were recent widows, both young and older and with no children. For the most part, the women looked gaunt and tired. Some were disheveled of dress and hair. Others were wringing their hands and sitting in postures of isolation. Some pulled at their skirts or picked their lips. How could these women, who appeared distressed themselves, ever deal with nursing the sick and injured?

Many, though, also radiated a resolve I could not help but attribute to a possible need for retribution. Were they thinking volunteering could perhaps serve to atone for their losses or provide escape from pain? Where they patriotic, or did they hold religious convictions that stirred their commitment to God or country? I did not know and admitted to myself that I saw them only as possible competitors for what I believed to be a limited number of training opportunities.

My intentions were not as noble as what I perceived theirs to be. Did I want out of my present state of uselessness more than I wanted to specifically work as a nurse? Nursing would certainly make me useful, and so with that, my one noble thought, I soothed any guilt that might be lurking at the edges regarding my intentions. The truth was that I did want to help, to make a difference, and this seemed the perfect solution.

It was now past noon and still the doctor had not appeared. We were all fidgeting and restless, none more than me, and many needed to go to their jobs. Two women left for work, but the rest remained in their seats.

At two thirty, the doctor finally arrived, accompanied by a woman in a nursing uniform. The doctor's three-piece tweed suit was too warm for the balmy day, making him even redder in the face than he would have been naturally. Sparse gray hair framed his glistening ruddiness, and pince-nez spectacles rested low on his nose. He obviously knew he was far behind the scheduled time for his meeting with us. He did not apologize though and quickly began speaking in short, clipped phrases and, without any seeming emotion or passion, said what he had come to say. He was traveling up and down the country talking to women's groups to raise money for the hospitals and needed supplies, as well as recruiting volunteers for the actual training.

"Nurses for both existing and new hospitals are urgently being called into service across all of France," he said. "Some nurses finishing their initial training might be sent to mobile field hospital stations closer to the front. These locations move as the fighting moves and pose dangers from many sources, not the least of which are the Germans.

"The Red Cross needs women with a predisposed nature for nursing, which is complementary, of course, to your gender's feminine and maternal instincts," he added. He did not elaborate specifically with qualifying details and did not suffer many questions, as he abruptly turned the meeting over to his nurse to explain the specifics of training.

As he hurried off with a brisk step, I wondered where he would go next, where he doctored, and had he been at the front and was he going back again. He somehow did not foster the notion of a man "with a predisposed nature" for doctoring in such harsh circumstances as war, but I sensed he was very effective at raising money. Papa said wars ran on blood and money—the money was hard to start and the blood was hard to stop.

All attention now turned to the nurse. She was my height and appeared weary and solemn. I believed she knew firsthand about which she spoke. She told us stories and gave examples of what we would face in the understaffed and underequipped hospitals, some a significant distance from the fighting, as well as field facilities in close proximity to battlefield sites. She also said that the men we would be taking care of had serious injuries: limbs missing or hanging by tendon or ligament; sight gone from chemical gassings; holes blown through their bodies; injuries to their heads, both physical and mental; and relentless fevers accompanied far too often by raging infections. Some never spoke again before they passed, but for those who knew they were dying, we might also write letters for them to their loved ones. We would assist the doctors in whatever ways were needed, including triage and treating wounds. Some nurses would work alongside physicians during surgeries.

Then, with an absent look and as though the words found themselves spoken before she realized they had come from her mouth, she said, "You live and breathe blood and death, both awake and in your sleep. We can seldom wash away the red stains from our skin, much less from our uniforms. The sounds never leave your ears and the smells never leave your nose. Never in the history of wartime has the need for nurses been this great, for never in the history of combat have there been weapons of war so cruel and devastating."

As we sat in rapt attention, she painted a harsh reality of what we might experience on the journey toward becoming a wartime nurse. She said some hospitals required more of nurses than others; some of the men would be injured to a greater degree, and in such situations, the doctors and more experienced nurses would provide additional training once we were assigned to a post. The initial training was two months, after which we would receive our nursing diploma. For the advanced level of Auxiliary Nurse, an additional six months of hospital experience was required.

"Oh yes," she went on to say, as though an afterthought, "all training is paid for by the volunteer herself, and there are no wages attached to your service thereafter. Therefore, you must have some source of monies both to cover your training and your time in service. You will truly be volunteers, albeit trained volunteers, in every sense of the word." She paused, and we resumed breathing.

Four women stood and departed the room quietly. Six of us remained. We sat perfectly still, examining within ourselves if we could possibility do what might be expected. The nurse then asked for questions and answered each one with patience and almost an air of relief that we hadn't all up and fled.

After we seemed to exhaust all possible questions and had again gone quiet, the nurse passed around forms we were to take and complete. If, after a night of contemplation and talking with our loved ones, we were still interested, had sufficient funds, and wanted to volunteer, we would meet her the next morning at nine back in this same room. Only those truly committed to moving forward were to return, as the timelines to leave for training were short. Once we turned in our paperwork, she would immediately conduct an examination with each volunteer, discuss the training schedules, and assign us a training site. We would then purchase our train tickets and travel north to the training hospitals in and about Paris.

I swallowed hard. One day to decide.

If only Papa had been traveling, it would have been so much easier, I thought. Solange knew my heart, and after terse and then tender conversations over the past days, she had agreed to support my decision to volunteer. But facing Papa would be a different story, and I knew Solange dreaded it at least as much as I did. She would be blamed for my decision more than I.

Solange was waiting for me outside the church. As I paused in the doorway before walking down the steps to meet her, I watched her pacing back and forth, slowly wringing her hands in thought. She had been waiting all those hours. We went for tea at a nearby café.

Sitting in silence and avoiding each other's eyes, we sat surveying the people at surrounding tables. When our server came to greet us, we quickly and without having glanced at our choices told her we would have a pot of chamomile. Before our tea arrived, I began to share with Solange all the doctor and nurse had to say. I spoke slowly and precisely, hoping my words carried weight enough to be convincing. I knew I needed to present a face of strength to this commitment I did not altogether feel. My knees remained as weak as when I had risen from my chair at the meeting's end. But still I held her eyes and her hands in my own as I pleaded with her to support me. My decision had been made. I was going to do this.

After I finished speaking, she loosened my hands, leaned back in the chair, and looked round the café. Fighting tears in her eyes by blotting them away at the corners with her fingertips, she sat silent for many minutes. We were both taking time to compose ourselves before speaking further. I saw a softening in her dark eyes, and her face and body became lax with a decision made. She knew she must either assist me in what ways she could or break our bond of loving support. Over the years we often disagreed, but when one of us was sure about something with a great desire to see it accomplished, we were always there to support one another. This, however, was certainly a matter of considerable difference than a strong opinion about choosing tutors, dresses, or what our studies were to include. A different matter altogether. I inhaled deeply. Would she support me now?

"Let me approach Papa first. You have no chance of winning favor if you storm in and make demands. This requires tact and diplomacy rather than a clash of two strong wills. I hate that you are putting me in this position, Marie."

"I can be tactful when called for, and I do not need to hide behind your skirts, Solange! And in the end it doesn't matter how much Papa protests because I am going. And I am sorry you even feel compelled to become involved in a matter in which I know you truly side with Papa."

"You do not completely understand my sentiments, *soeur chèri*. There is a part of me that wants to hug you and enthusiastically tell you to go. I do understand you and am proud of you for wanting to do this. But out of love for you and out of my own dread of personal pain for Papa and myself I would never forgive myself if I agreed to such a thing and then it turned out horribly. Can you understand that?"

"Yes, of course," I said, exhaling all my held breath. "The last thing I desire is to inflict worry or pain upon you and Papa. You must know that as well. But do we sacrifice a life that could be better lived only to live a life lost—without meaning or risk?"

"Marie," she said, taking my hand, "just let me talk to Papa first."

We left the café and walked home in silence, arm in arm and more slowly than usual, prolonging the meeting with Papa and gleaning strength from our tight hold on one another.

The truth was that I was relieved at Solange's offer to speak with Papa before I made my request. She was right, of course, that I would have demanded that Papa acquiesce, insisting there was nothing he could do to stop me. Solange would be able to say the same but with finesse. I did want Papa to understand; more than anything I wanted to be sent away with his blessing and not his wrath.

Once we were home and shed our thin wraps (as slowly as possible, I might add), we walked to Papa's study to find him still there. To my great chagrin he appeared not to have moved from his chair, and his desk did not seem any tidier than when we had left him that morning. His elbows were on the desktop with his large head cradled facedown into his hands.

This was not a good time. But I knew there would never truly be a good time. Solange and I exchanged a glance in acknowledgment of these facts, and I held back just outside the door as she asked if she might enter and have a word.

Pulling himself together, his posture now erect but his features still lined with unease and weariness, Papa quickly responded, "Of course, *ma chère.* Come in. I am nearly finished here."

Solange left the door slightly ajar, leaving enough room that I might stand outside, not quite seen but able to hear. She spoke slowly and quietly as she reminded Papa of our thrice-weekly volunteer efforts with the Red Cross. She told him about the announcement earlier in the week seeking volunteer nurses, and that I had been curious and so had attended this meeting, which we were now returning from. "Papa, Marie is of a mind that she is wanting to consider the opportunity to serve as a volunteer nurse."

At this, he sat up even straighter. Solange now had his undivided attention. "A nurse? Marie wants to become a nurse? What kind of a nurse?"

"Well, I am sure you are aware that there is a great need for nurses to serve with the Red Cross. The Red Cross is here in Marseille this week seeking funding for hospitals, supplies, and volunteers to be trained as nurses. They would provide the training and then the nurse would work in a hospital assisting in the treatment and care of the wounded. This is what Marie is considering."

I quickly glanced into the room. His head dropped once again into his hands as he struggled to compose himself. Without lifting his head, he said, "Yes, I know of the need. I know of the training and I know of the risk. What I did not know was that such a thing was being considered within our family!"

I rounded the door and entered the room with as much confidence in my carriage and voice as I could command. "This would not be an act of family sedition, Papa, but rather a fulfillment of a growing desire to move beyond what I have come to see as a stagnant life. I am restless and wanting more! Have you not seen that in me, Papa? Can you not understand at all?"

"Yes, Marie. I have seen you growing discontent, and I know the restlessness. It is my companion as well." He pushed back his chair from the desk and slowly rose and walked over to the window. "Do you feel a strong call toward nursing?" he asked as I looked at his back.

"I don't know, but I do feel a strong call to be away and to offer service. I am young, strong, and I have little fear," I replied with strong resolution.

Without turning around, he said quietly, "When have you ever had to face fear, my little one? My life has been devoted to assuring that you and Solange would never have cause to fear or doubt for your safety and well-being. And now you tell me you want to willingly place yourself in harm's way?"

His shoulders rose as his voice took on a deeper timbre. He was making quite an effort to prevent the conversation from escalating to a place without reason. "You know the train station also needs volunteers in the canteen and even the infirmary. Would you not consider this?"

I saw the hope in his eyes as he turned around to face us, that maybe I had not considered it but would think it a viable alternative to my request. I sighed. "Papa, my heart's desire is to do this. I have the papers with me, and I am asking, imploring you to please sign them and allow me this freedom." I pulled the papers from behind my skirt and held them out to him.

He looked intensely into my eyes. "Freedom is a long road fraught on the way with hazards, temptations, and unexpected detours toward what we least expect. It seldom takes us where we thought we were going. Is this the journey you ask that I acquiesce to?"

I nodded. "Yes. I am asking that when I leave it is with the knowledge that you trust me enough to use the good judgment I have learned from you. That you acknowledge, as Solange and I do when you leave, that we always come home to one another."   Knowing he would attempt to persuade me otherwise, I had rehearsed these last sentences repeatedly in my head and delivered them with as much confidence as I could muster.

"If you were my son, you would be off in the trenches, and I would have naught to say about it. As it is, you are as spirited as any father might wish a son to be. Having daughters, I have always felt a deep sense of relief that I would never have to send a child of mine to war. And here I find, again, the best of plans thwarted by what I cannot control. Do you realize that the truth is you are incredibly naïve, without any benefit of the realities that await you?" He turned to the window once more, and I barely heard him say, "But then, neither do our young men as we send them away with shouts of victory and acclaim their great valor."

After what seemed an interminable silence, he walked toward me and placed his big hands on my shoulders and with an audible sigh said, "I only ask, Marie, that you pledge to me you will keep safe and out of harm's way whenever you possibly have the choice. God knows I have lost too many women that I have loved. I do not think I could bear it again." Shaking me a little as though to truly sink this caution into my soul, he asked, "Do you understand what I am saying, dear daughter?"

I understood. It would break his heart if I did not come home, as it would break ours if he ever did the same. "Yes, Papa. I understand more than you could possibly know."

At that moment I only wanted to bury my head into his broad chest and relinquish all my plans, staying there safe and sound in our home in Marseille.

CHAPTER 4

THE BATTLES, VERDUN, APRIL 1916 – DECEMBER 1916

I was sure my eyes were open, but I neither saw nor heard anything. Nothing at all. Fearing I had died in the night from the shelling, I jumped from my cot. When my feet found the floor and I knew I was still alive, I grabbed my cape and flung open the tent flap.

The morning was shrouded in heavy, damp fog. The smell of spent munitions hung thick in the air. I knew I would always remember that odor of sulfur and fear. And blood. Always the iron-tinged smell of blood I could never completely remove from myself. In what was becoming a chronic behavior I could not seem to stop, I rubbed my hands up and down, up and down the front of my uniform, which I had slept in again. At least the night before I had taken off the soiled apron and hung it across a stool. I would put a clean one on before the day truly started.

Looking at my almost-clean hands and arms, I knew I must have managed a quick washing before collapsing into sleep. Though perpetually stained pink, my hands were free from the red stickiness. I must trim my nails again tonight, I thought. Close trimming of my nails and brush-scrubbing of my hands were the only ways I ever hoped to remove the remnants of carnage.

I seldom distinguished one day from another as the beginnings and endings and in-betweens were so similar; there was no sense of time passing—only the constant movement of bodies between battle, triage, treatment, or burial. As I tied on a fresh apron, I ticked off in my head what I thought were yesterday's numbers. Twenty surgeries were not uncommon in a day, but I thought yesterday we had done even more. Twenty-five, perhaps thirty.

The other nurses on my team, Jeanne and Annette, were already gone from our tent. It was early still, and they had allowed me to sleep just a little later. The three of us worked side by side in the triage and surgery. We had trained together in Paris for nine months before leaving for Verdun, having been chosen to travel to the front as part of the surgical team for Dr. Claude Bisset. He had previously set up several surgical teams in other field hospitals but then returned to Paris to continue training others. Our team, however, was intended to have him as its surgeon. He would not be returning this time to Paris.

We were posted to a field hospital west of Verdun, some distance away from the trenches and the fighting. Jeanne, Annette, and I, as Dr. Bisset's nursing team, were often the recipients of both his praise and his frustration. We were dedicated to the skilled doctor, and our months of intense training in Paris had forged a tight bond of loyalty and friendship between us. We were all on edge from the persistent fatigue and helplessness of losing many men to the ravages of brutal wounds. Their limbs were often blown off their bodies and their bones shattered beyond salvaging. Amputations, though performed frequently and as quickly as possible, did not always result in saving the soldier who frequently had other sites of severe injury. Infection was the soldier's other enemy. Yesterday had ended badly, with Dr. Bisset and other doctors taking their irritation out on their nurses—again.

Before retiring for the night, my two colleagues and I, in the semi-privacy of our tent, shared openly our own complaints.

"I am sick of their ranting dismissals! Their arrogance is insufferable! How dare they even insinuate that today was made worse by any 'inefficiencies' on our part?" I was furious as I stormed round the tent, rubbing my hands up and down my bloody apron front.

"Easy, easy, Marie," said Annette in a calm, even voice. "It is only their fear talking."

"We are all afraid! That is no excuse for their verbal attacks." I seethed with indignation.

"But they are afraid also of us," said Annette as she flopped down onto her cot.

"Nurses? Doctors afraid of nurses?"

"Not of nurses. Of women. We are seeing our men, our heroes, naked, bleeding, screaming in agony, and dying by the dozens. And the ones who are to snatch them from the precipice of death, our great doctors, are helpless in the face of such slaughter. Neither these soldiers nor our doctors were ever to be brought to such a place. Now, because they have been and are frightened beyond anything they could have imagined, they place their fear and humiliation upon us. They cannot bear it, you see. But by our presence and forced calmness, we give evidence to their shame. The denigration of war has made frail minds of us all. But in the minds of men, we have always been frail and therefore must be so now— and blamed for their frailty as well."

I was stopped and stunned by Annette's explanation. I sat down on my cot across from her. "I think after this is all over, Annette, you must become a philosopher. Or perhaps a psychologist. Do you really think what you say can be true?"

"Oh, most definitely! My father was a physician, and when he lost patients or his treatments were not effective, my mother, brother, and I always received the blunt end of his fear of incompetence. Many a late dinner was passed with my father ranting about our laziness, our lack of ambition, our not being appreciative of how hard he worked, and on and on. We learned to keep quiet and eat quickly. This is no different. We must work as well as we can and hold our counsel."

"Keeping my counsel is not always easy for me. I wanted to throw a bloody limb across the table and hit them squarely in their heads," I countered.

"Well, remember that as women we have always been the weak ones, the gender to be sheltered and pitied. The ones needing care and nurturing. War has torn the mantle of masculinity from the shoulders of our men, and we reinforce their dependence on us as we work alongside them and bloody our hands in ways they believe were not meant for women. They all feel that women could not possibly cope with such horrific realities. I dream of the day when this is over that our service will be recognized, that our role in working with the doctors at the front will result in opportunities beyond what we have now at home. We will have proven we are capable. For after this war, I am going to become a surgeon and take over my father's practice. Won't he be surprised?" Annette finished this last thought with a smile across her lips as she lay down on her cot, pulled her blanket up over her, and, as she did each night regardless of the day's events, quickly went to sleep.

Throughout our training and our work together at the front, I had never heard Annette share such thoughts and ideas. But I knew I agreed with her. We were not seen as equals but as capable assistants at best. And at worst, necessary appendages providing a third, fourth, or fifth hand to the doctor frantically attempting to stem the flow of blood and wipe clean the area to be cut into, removed, sewn, and bandaged.

On most days, looking beyond fatigue, anger, and frustration, I did know that Dr. Bisset respected our work with him. I held him in great esteem and wanted the same level of respect from him in return. I realized my anger was most likely my wanting his approval and that this desire lay at the heart of my unease at the end of such difficult days. I too hoped to continue my work once this nightmare ended. I had dreams of returning to the hospital in Paris and continuing to work alongside Dr. Bisset in surgery. We had learned much from the dying and desperate. The need for quick action to save what lives we could forced us, allowed us to attempt, in the moment between saving or losing a patient, extreme methods we would not have tried in the sterile surgical suites in the hospitals of Paris. I wanted something good to come from this mad, surreal experience. Something I could take back and make sense of. Something so I could look Papa in the eyes and say, "Yes, it was worth it, for I learned to be a better nurse. A better person. Someone who, in a saner world, can make a difference." And with that thought I also lay down on my cot and drifted off to sleep.

The next five months, from June through November, proceeded in much the same vein. The shellings, gassings, and trench fighting continued as we tended the never-ending flow of wounded and dying men. Depending on the direction of the fighting, we sometimes moved our hospital site farther to the west or the south. Ambulances and trucks would roar in, and we would pack and load hastily to a new field of operation. In late November, we received word that we would need to move once again. But the doctors, conferring with the military in command close to our site, decided that the battle, so widespread around Verdun, was waning. France was pushing back the Germans, the end was near, and they felt it safe if we remained at our current location, where it was determined we were most needed. Thus we stayed and triaged, treated, and operated, sending those seriously injured but deemed stable to travel on the medical trains west to the hospitals in Paris. Those we judged as too weak to travel remained within our field hospital, and we cared for them as best we could. Many died. Some of the soldiers recovered enough after treatment or minor surgery that they returned directly to the trenches. Infection was rampant, and I knew that many who rejoined their stations of duty, even if they survived another round of warfare, would ultimately die from infection.

In early December, I woke up more disoriented than ever, not wanting to move and then realizing I was actually unable to move. My body felt hot and wet, the breeze drifting over me causing prickles of chills as sweat and blood dripped into my eyes, nose, and mouth.

The familiar and constant battlefield smells of sulfur, blood, and feces washed through my nostrils more intensely than usual. The sounds of moaning were close and punctuated by screams. I could do nothing but lie still with eyes closed, barely breathing, and tasting what I knew to be my own blood. I willed myself calm and tried to take account of my senses. Cold. It was so cold. I knew I was on the ground and that I was injured. In flashes, I remembered running from our tents as fiery blasts hit close all around us during the night.

I continued to be still, eyes clamped tightly shut, dreading with every fiber of my being the condition in which I might find my body and the bodies of those surely sprawled around me should I open my eyes. Maybe I was dying. Maybe I would die and be free of all this. With that thought, I drifted off again from consciousness. Whether minutes or hours passed before I awoke, I couldn't know. I knew only it was dark, as I could perceive no hint of light through my closed lids. The night was full of low moans and the occasional sounds of weeping. I needed to open my eyes, thankful that it was nighttime. Opening my eyes to a darkened reality might allow me to gradually return to a semblance of sanity. And I thought I could move.

In great pain, I managed to sit up and look about in the complete darkness. Overcast and extremely cold, no stars illuminated the space around me. The darkness was a gift for which I cried grateful tears. I knew I was in shock and felt no discomfort in my legs. Thinking I might attempt to stand, I found them not willing to assist in any manner as pain ripped through the rest of my body. My arms steadied me back into a sitting position, but that lasted only a minute or so. Dizzy from the effort, I lay down on my back and turned my head from side to side in an attempt to see what was left of us all and our makeshift hospital. I could see nothing. Even as my eyes adjusted to the dark, I saw no tents, no equipment, no one about to come and help. No one at all. The sound of my own weeping joined the chorus of the wounded I knew were all about me. Some of us had survived. With that thought hung like a thin thread of hope round my heart, I drifted again into oblivion.

They said I fought well. I battled the infection that had seeped into the wounds in my legs and traveled through my body, bringing fevers and fits of chills. My left leg had been broken and both limbs torn open in deep gashes running the length of my calves. One hundred stitches in each leg. The broken leg was kept splinted instead of cast so the long seam of stitches could heal more quickly. A severe concussion kept me in and out of reality for three weeks. During periods of wakefulness I spoke not a word. I had no thoughts, could not formulate questions, and wanted only to go to sleep again. No one mentioned Dr. Bisset, Annette, or Jeanne. If I did not ask, they would not be obliged to answer.

December through February was spent in the recovery ward of the Pitié-Salpêtrière Hospital, in Paris, the same one in which I had trained. My physical wounds were healing well, and I was encouraged to take short walks several times a day. I did so with the aid of crutches and the kind assistance from the nurses. Still speaking little, only one or two words at a time and perhaps only once or twice each day, I was told repeatedly there would be no long-term consequences from the concussion and that once I began normal conversation again, I would be well on my way to full recovery and able to travel home to Marseille.

In March of 1917, Dr. Geoffrey Renard, who was assigned to my care and had provided such with great compassion and diligence, came to pay me what he said was "a serious visit" to assess my readiness to return home. He could find no medical reason for my lack of ability to speak more than a few words and requested that I try.

"It is most important to your recovery," he said, "that you begin to speak openly and honestly about your condition and what you are feeling. Only then can I help address your concerns."

I did not think any of the staff had realized I had "concerns." And what was this about my "condition"? I had recovered from the concussion and was close to walking independently, which meant they would soon send me home—the place I did not want to go, for I would be appearing on Papa's doorstep a wounded and broken person. I could not go there without at least some kind of normalcy returned to my spirit as well as my body. Thoughts of Papa and Solange's distress at seeing me return impaired—defeated—were more grievous to me than any pain I now suffered.

With a huge sigh of resignation and some sense of relief, I then began to talk. Where were Dr. Bisset, Jeanne, and Annette? Were they all right? How many others were injured? How long had I been here, what month was it, had they contacted my family, and could I please stay on and work in the hospital?

Gently, Dr. Renard disclosed that all three of my colleagues had been killed in the shelling, along with four others who worked with us in the hospital and all but one of the wounded soldiers. The remaining survivors of that day had already recovered enough to be sent home or to care facilities—except me. The decision had been made soon after my arrival at the hospital to keep me at the facility in which I had trained—a familiar environment with people sensitive to what had occurred. And, yes, my family knew I had been injured, that I was recovering and would soon be in contact with them regarding my plans for a homecoming. We would talk later about my remaining in Paris to work in the hospital.

With a furrowed brow, Dr. Renard shook his finger at me. "For the next two weeks you must do exactly as you are instructed. Eat what the nurses bring, and I mean all of it, exercise as much as possible by walking around the ward, and engage others in conversation. Come back to life, Marie, and if at the end of the two weeks you can convince me you are able to begin nursing again, we will see what positions are available. Oh, and you *must* contact your father and sister within the next few days. They are desperately worried for you."

Without hesitation I agreed to comply with each point. The possibility of resuming my work here, and not returning posthaste to Marseille, served as positive motivation. I was overcome with grief at the loss of my colleagues but betrayed nothing of my heavy heart to this physician who held my precarious future in his hands. I thanked him and bid him what I hoped was a hearty farewell, then fell back into my bed and wrapped my sorrow round me tightly along with my blankets. Today I would grieve the loss of my friends, and tomorrow I would begin again. I knew I could do this. I must do this, I thought, for otherwise I would be sent home.

CHAPTER 5

NURSING IN PARIS, DECEMBER 1916 – DECEMBER 1919

The end of March found me standing alone on my own mended legs. Crutches gone and with only a slight limp, I pleaded with Dr. Renard and the hospital's administration to allow me to resume my duties as a nurse. They knew me well, knew my determination and my skills, and I think they knew also that continuing my work was a way to continue my healing. They also understood I was not ready to go home. Two weeks into April, I was cleared to return to part-time floor nursing. Both legs would ache by the end of my shortened shifts, but the pain was a paltry nuisance in exchange for remaining in Paris with my fellow nurses and friends. I wrote to Papa and Solange of my continued gains toward full recovery as evidenced by having returned to my professional duties. This would reassure them, as it did me, that I would be whole again.

I stayed at la Pitié-Salpêtrière, where I was most needed, and during the next almost-three years, the soldiers and their blood continued to flow through the surgical suites. In June of 1918, I returned to full-time shifts and was placed in surgical recovery, where I tended the just-repaired-and-put-back-together. I found this easy work, though somewhat tedious compared with my duties at the front, where the pace was furious and there was little time to think of anything but the injured in front of me.

Soon I was requesting to assist in surgery. There was regular turnover of nurses coming and going, and I reminded my supervisors again and again of my field experience. They assured me they didn't need reminding. They knew I possessed the skills. However, what none of us were sure of was whether I was emotionally ready to return to the intensity of participating in surgeries.

By the end of July, after much convincing of both myself and others, I secured the night surgery shift. I approached that first night back with great anticipation, pushing aside any hesitation I might have felt as to whether I was prepared for what was always the theatre of the unexpected.

Halfway through the patient's amputation sweating and dizziness began. I heard voices—people shouting, screams inside my head—and felt an overwhelming urgency to run. Run as quickly as possible away from the blood and the screams before I vomited or fainted, or both. I was escorted from the surgery suite. Another nurse took me to the recovery area where I had spent so much time tending those in similar distress. As my breathing slowed, my feelings of panic ebbed as well.

Mon Dieu! My God, I was so embarrassed. I felt ashamed and humiliated and felt such a sense of failure that at that moment I wanted nothing more than to be anywhere besides my beloved hospital. A nurse that could not nurse! A professional that could not pull herself together to do what she had been trained to do and had done so well. Before, that is. Before this place my mind now went to and always of its own accord. A place I knew I was still running from. How would I escape these horrible episodes of the past and return to the present? I felt I was going insane.

The next week I spent in my room in the nurses' dormitory and left only for meals and scheduled appointments with Dr. Renard, who spent thirty minutes each day talking with me about my panic in surgery. My flashbacks were not really specific individual memories but rather a compilation of the horrible sights and sounds I had experienced, exploding in my head. I came to realize that my need to remain busy, even frantic and overly fatigued, stemmed from my fear that those moments of panic lay close to the surface, waiting to overflow by a trigger that might catch me unawares. Long work hours, consistent routine, and constant fatigue formed the dam that kept the panic contained.

My compassionate physician-counselor explained that many serving on the battlefields came home with what the medical profession was calling *neurasthénie* or "neurasthenia." I later learned this emotional state was more commonly referred to as *une crise de tristesse sombre*: "a crisis of black melancholy." He assured me there was no need for shame, that I only needed to be patient with myself and allow my mind and spirit time to continue healing. With time, he explained, I would no longer feel the panic and fear or the utter despair that occasionally came over me as well. After a week of such discussions, I told him I would understand if they requested I give up my position at the hospital and return to Marseille.

"On the contrary, Marie," Dr. Renard said as he sat back in his chair looking thoughtfully at me. "We were rather hoping you would consider two positions here. One would be your assistance in the surgery suite, but only when the doctor is ready to close the wound site, and the other in the ward where the men are suffering similar concerns as yours but to a much greater degree. Your patients would then benefit by both your nursing skills and your understanding of these secondary after-effects of battle."

"While I am very appreciative of this offer, Doctor, I will need a few days' time to consider if I am capable of what you are asking," I responded. I was still so shaken from what had occurred during surgery that I was not sure I could return there under any circumstances. And I was certainly unsure as to whether I desired to attend patients who would remind me every day of my own struggles. What if it happened again during an operation or made my own situation worse by attempting to care for those "suffering similar concerns," as the doctor had explained?

"Give it some thought. Let's continue to meet each day this next week. I think you will find that by discussing and facing your fears you will eventually lay them to rest. After next week, think about resuming your position in surgical recovery only. Gradually, as you feel you are able, you might begin to enter the surgery suite just as an observer and then, depending on those results, perhaps assist the surgeons with closings again. You must decide what it is you most want to do, and then together we can move forward. All must be done slowly but can be achieved with patience and courage. I know you have both." He stood, took my elbow, and ushered me to the door. I returned to my room, my head flooded with new thoughts.

Why, after my display of panic, would the physicians still want me to participate in any aspect of surgery, let alone in closing a patient's surgery site? It was because of my stitching. My years of needlework—pulling thread in and out of light and heavy material in rows of small, precise, tight stitches—proved of great benefit in surgery. I had a gift for suturing. I could sew a wound or surgery site together with great speed and accuracy and in neat stitches that left only a narrow, straight scar. And because of my strict and consistent practice of sterilizing everything that came in contact with the patient, those I put back together seldom had secondary infections. For these reasons, I was in great demand in the surgery suites.

Eventually, I did reenter the operating room, but only at the end of a procedure, when my sewing skills were needed. I also resumed my work in surgical recovery and would, on most days, be called into the surgery suite once or twice each shift to assist in closing. However, I did not acquiesce to working in the sanatorium ward. I convinced myself it was too far a physical distance from the surgery ward where I might be needed at short notice to complete a site closure. It was much more efficient, I reasoned with myself and my supervisors, if I remained working in surgical recovery where I could move in and out of surgery as quickly as needed.

Dr. Renard seemed to understand my reticence and did not argue with my logic regarding efficiency, although he did request that we continue to meet one hour per week. We did, and I found I both dreaded and anticipated those sessions. During our conversations, my pain would rise to the surface where it had to be acknowledged, and occasionally, catching me surprised but ultimately relieved, it rose above and out of me. It seemed unending, this acknowledgment and purging of the past. The doctor was encouraging, told me I was doing well, and that with time the painful memories would be completely dispelled, and I would be free. I chose to believe him and strived to recount and release whatever came into my mind. Once I was empty, I believed, it would be over.

There were many other nurses and physicians at the hospital who also had worked at the front in various field hospitals. We formed a close-knit community and spent most of our off-hours together walking Paris and taking our meals in small cafés about the city. We did not spend our time reliving the past but talked only of the present and even more about the future. We all wanted to move forward but were holding fast to the security the hospital work provided us, both in terms of our careers and as a familiar, safe environment in which to think about what we might do when the world was sane again.

The lively, often intense conversations with my close nursing friends would move from the hilarious to the more serious as we spoke excitedly about the future of modern medicine, equality, and the eventual vote for women; what we wanted to do; where we would live; and where we might travel. We never spoke of whom we might love or when we would actually be going back to our families.

Though often difficult to put pen to paper, I faithfully wrote to Solange and Papa several times a week. Solange's letters and mine flew with regularity between Paris and Marseille. After a time, she stopped asking when I might be coming home, stopped telling me about the openings at the hospital in Marseille where I could "easily find work," and began filling her letters with anecdotes from home. I had shared only vague brushstrokes of my journey regarding my physical and emotional recovery, and I appreciated her patience as I continued to be patient with myself. Eventually, I returned to where I truly felt I belonged as a nurse—in the operating rooms assisting the surgeons. I kept the memories and feelings of despair and panic pushed back deep into the recesses of my mind. I did my job and did it well and considered myself quite repaired.

I always knew I would return to Marseille, but it would have to be in my own time, when I felt prepared to face those I had not seen for several years now.

And they would need to perhaps prepare to face a grown and changed Marie. Someone they might not know as well as they assumed. For she was someone different.

With the war's end in November of 1918, our last patients were eventually discharged and, thankfully, no more soldiers arrived to fill those beds. Now able to look toward their own futures, many of the physicians, nurses, and staff began to take their leave. I stayed on another year, but at the beginning of December 1919, feeling mostly recovered and therefore with some restored confidence, I submitted my resignation to the hospital and began packing my trunk. I wrote Solange and Papa to expect me home by the end of December. The mailing of this letter was accompanied by feelings of profound homesickness as well as deep fear for what might await me. Await us all.

I had carried my nursing diploma to the front with me, and it was lost in the destruction along with so many other precious items. On my last day before leaving Paris, my friends, fellow nurses, and even many of the physicians surprised me with a final fête and awarded me a diploma of Advanced Auxiliary Nurse. In an attached letter signed by the hospital's supervising physician, a summary recounted the history of my training, beginning at that same hospital in 1915, my service during the war in the field hospitals, my assignment specific to Verdun, and completion of the advanced nurse's training following injuries sustained on the battlefront. My appreciation was beyond my ability to express in mere words, and I was not ashamed of my tears. They were close friends and exceptional colleagues, and I would miss them dearly.

A military representative presented me with a pin he attached to my uniform as acknowledgement of my service to France as a Red Cross Nurse and specifically for my service during the Battle of Verdun. Once again, I was speechless and much pleased. At that moment, I felt all was well. All was healed. I knew Papa would be proud of me.

To say that it was difficult to leave the hospital, my patients and dear friends and colleagues, was an understatement. After many hugs and tears, I boarded the train mid-afternoon in late December, the snow falling heavily on my navy-blue wool nurse's cloak. I was wearing my uniform home with my accomplishments pinned on my front for all to see. I was returning to Papa and Solange having accomplished what I had intended: finding my own way and hopefully myself in the process. But I had no idea of the self that awaited me in Marseille.

CHAPTER 6

HOME AND THEN HOME, DECEMBER 1919 – APRIL 1920

I arrived home just before the winter holidays. Papa and Solange welcomed me with much affection and quiet relief. It seemed I was never to be out of Solange's sight those first few weeks back inside our house. Elise, our beloved cook and confidant, had moved to Avignon, in 1916, and taken up residence with her widowed daughter and grandchildren. Solange had assumed meal preparation duties, attempting not too successfully to replicate Elise's recipes, and continuously coaxed me to eat. She also did my laundry, prepared my baths, and washed my hair. While I understood it was her way of reassuring herself that I was safe and sound and truly home, as well as wanting to make me feel welcomed and cared for, it was disconcerting at best.

I felt a great settling in at the core of my soul to be back in our home, my room, and with those I loved so dearly. At the same time, I also felt very much a visitor; while understandable after more than four years away, I wondered when I would again feel at home in our house.

Those first months of 1920 (actually through that winter into spring) I was content to remain with my family, keeping much to myself. Solange and I went to the markets once or twice a week and prepared our meals together, eating quietly with Papa when he was home, but I was not eager for further social interaction. Time and again I turned down the many well-intentioned invitations from both old friends or newer friends of Solange's who now wanted me to join in their many activities. Explanations regarding my continued fatigue and weariness, quiet and rest being what was needed for a while longer to restore me to myself, always accompanied my regrets. And this was certainly true and everyone understood, but the real reason was that I desired only solitude. Within that solitude I found a place of largesse that became my center, and I did not venture beyond that. Indeed, I found myself retreating more deeply into a confusing despair as the weeks passed.

Apart from social invitations, no one asked anything of me. No one seemed curious as to what I had been doing as a nurse during those four years of war or what my experiences had been. Certainly no one asked what my plans were now that I had returned home. I later learned that Solange had told everyone not to make any inquiries of me.

Social discussions focused primarily on which husbands and young men had and had not returned home, who was and was not pregnant, the high prices and scarcity of all goods, and other post-war gossip that inspired these women's conversations. Most wives were now out of the working environment, solely restored to their domestic duties and, I assumed, attempting to become pregnant and repopulate our country. The official decree often heard from the government was that women could now return to "their rightful places."

During the infrequent times when I was with Solange and her acquaintances, conversation almost certainly came round to the topic of "greater equality for women." To my ears, these conversations often sounded loud and contentious. Now that the war was over, it was evident that women had served ably in so many capacities. Many of my sister's friends held to the belief that men could no longer dispute the role their wives, sisters, and mothers had played in France's victory. Women had successfully replaced men in the factories and shops, served as nurses at the front, been drivers in the military, and on and on. Some of the women expressed the desire to continue working, and many were unwilling to give up their jobs just because their husbands were home.

I pretended to listen, nodded when I thought it appropriate, and offered no comments, for in truth, I had nothing to say that would relate to the present concerns of these women. Their eager post-war enthusiasm left me drained and seeking escape as soon as possible. After what I deemed as time enough spent in their company to be polite, and with a look of understanding from Solange, I would either walk home alone or, if we were entertaining in our home, retreat quietly upstairs.

My painting room, where I had spent so many wondrous hours in what seemed so long ago, was just as I had left it. The windows let in all the sun possible in those days of late winter. Sitting in my familiar chair under the windows, the rays warming me, gave me reason to hope that the words I used to assure others of my well-being would become my truth. That I would soon be filled with energy and some renewal of vigor. That room became my place of retreat, but the smells of the oils and turpentine seemed unfamiliar. The bright paintings stacked against the walls could not possibly have been created by me, and although I picked up the clean brushes and stroked the soft bristles, moved here and there the paint-stained spatulas, and pushed my fingers one by one into the dried paint on the palate, I could not imagine inspiration would ever cause me to lift brush to canvas again.

I passed many hours there in the long-familiar chair, facing away from the window toward the center of the room. Occasionally, I would attempt to read, but the pages never held my attention and I often dozed off. Solange would bring me tea, sometimes sitting with me for brief chats, but mostly she left me alone.

After those first few weeks home under her watchful eye and having restored some meat to my bones, she left me to myself to "sort things out." When Papa was home, I made more of an effort to join the family. I convinced myself he had no worries regarding what he referred to as my "readjustment." And whenever I excused myself early from after-dinner conversation with those two I loved best, he would rise from his chair, embrace me gently, and comment that anyone could see I was still "ghastly tired." I knew that by this time Solange was beginning to suspect there was more to my retreating than just fatigue.

Solange and I each slept in our own rooms. Grown women would, of course.

During my first month home with nothing to fill my mind or tire my body, the little I did sleep was anything but restful. Then the nightmares began. Many nights I awoke in Solange's arms, shaking with fear and soaked in my own sweat, chilled to the bone. Screams of terror accompanied each episode that brought her running to my room. She spoke quiet words assuring me I was safe at home, and nothing could hurt me now. She would sometimes stay with me until first light or until I fell back asleep. I would awake many hours later, alone, and wonder if the nightmares had been real and whether Solange had actually come to care for me in the night. We never spoke of those frequent nighttime occurrences.

I began to dread going to sleep, knowing what was on the other side of wakefulness. I suffered guilt as well, aware that my nighttime terrors now involved my sister. She was becoming fatigued from worry and her own lack of sleep. After a while, as we both finished our nightly preparations for bed, she began coming to my room, where we would sit together talking quietly for some time. Rather than wait to comfort me in the midst of terrible dreams, she gently broached the subject of our experiences over the four years apart.

We shared together night after night, week upon week, and what we told one another were not the inconsequential, tepid comments in our letters shared during our separation. Those letters functioned as safe lifelines keeping us connected but never revealed anything that would cause worry or concern. Now, we were truly safe, together once more, and could both let loose four years of unspoken truths and talk heart to heart of the ravages of war and the price that had been paid.

Solange, knowing intuitively that what I had experienced, as evidenced by the night terrors, would be hard for me to disclose, began first to share. She slowly unraveled all that had occurred in our city of Marseille during those years—the devastation of so many families as word came of the loss of a husband, a father, a brother, a son. Some nurses from town lost their lives as well. With so many of the men gone, businesses and shops had to close. There were extreme food and fuel shortages, and mothers with no way to provide for themselves or their children were helped by those who could. With Papa's full support, my sister was at the heart of those efforts, keeping many widows and children warm and féd. She talked about the people we knew and cared about—those lost, those who came home, the ones who came home but never completely returned. And on and on she shared.

As Solange listened, I talked about my work close to the battlefields at the field hospital sites and the years nursing again in Paris before I came home. I spoke as well about my nurse friends, the doctors, and the patients lost in the war and those at the hospital in Paris I came to care about so deeply. We laughed and cried together, but even greater was the sense of relief that came with honest reflection. Honesty with one another and, more importantly, with ourselves. I thought of Dr. Renard and his encouraging me to put into words my feelings and impressions from those experiences.

Little by little, the war years were relived between us. Our nights of sharing and letting go became our own private world in which we found acceptance, release, and reconnection. We would begin talking as soon as dark fell and speak through much of the night, either in my bed or hers, and then sleep late into the morning.

She told me that shortly after I left, Papa suffered "an attack," and for months his memory seemed confused, his speech sometimes slurred, and his limbs were weak. Our longtime physician assured her that with rest and good care he would most likely recover his faculties, but he needed to begin to lighten his business obligations. During the many months of his recovery, Solange dealt with the management of the business. Papa did recover, but he forbade her to write me of this difficult period. I knew what she did not say: that worry for me most certainly contributed to his stress at that time and possibly to what I assumed had been a small stroke.

Since I had been home, I saw no evidence that Papa was anything but healthy—certainly grayer and a little more "stove up" in his joints, as he would comment, but still my same Papa. Solange retained her business responsibilities even after Papa resumed work to both lessen his stress and allow her to keep a close watch on him. She enjoyed the work and found she had a keen sense for it. In my absence, she had truly become a business partner with Papa in every sense of the word.

During the war years, their lives were hectic with business, community concerns, and perpetual worry regarding my safety. Papa relentlessly sought information from the northern front from any source he could; the news did nothing to dispel their fears. As the Battle of Verdun began and raged through those long months, they were terrified that I would not survive, as they knew I was in the middle of it.

My sister's revelations provided me a safe segue into what became my revisiting of all that had happened to me during that time. I told her about the deaths of Dr. Bisset, Jeanne, and Annette. About the smells, the sounds, the blood, the shells, the wounds, the surgeries, and the men I hoped we saved and those we could not. I told her of my daily fear and worry, and of my anger. I was surprised myself that anger rose up as bitter bile when I spoke to Solange of the devastation of war: the slaughter of the men, men on all sides of the conflict, and what I so strongly believed was the futility of it all. Whenever I became overly distressed and began wiping my hands up and down, up and down my nightdress, as I had at the front, Solange would take hold of them and calm me. After weeks of these nightly discussions, my nightmares became less frequent. I even started to sometimes sleep through the night.

During February I wrote letters to Dr. Bisset's family and to the parents of Jeanne and Annette. My missives were long and much overdue, but it was only those many years later that it was possible for me to extend to them my condolences. I continued to miss my colleagues and friends terribly, and they were often in my dreams. They were gone and I was left, having no idea of what was to become of me.

As the malaise that I had brought home gradually lightened and began to allow room for contemplation, stirrings of my old restlessness began to seep into my consciousness. I did not feel ready to resume hospital work again and, truth be told, did not want to fall into the predictable life in Marseille with the same familiar people. I did not have the energy or the will to become what was expected of me.

As the winter of 1919 was coming to an end, I saw in those around me an eagerness for a spring that assumed the world was in a peaceful place. Surrounded by this sliver of hope that I did not share, I began to feel even more uncomfortably out of place. I continued my smiles and nods, assuring everyone that of course I was feeling almost ready to resume "my old life" and would soon be inquiring into a nursing position at our hospital. They all smiled and nodded agreeably in return.

Of course, Solange was never fooled, and I was honest with her in every regard as to my current state of body and mind. She knew I was still fragile in many ways and not the least interested in working at our local hospital. Moreover, I had no inclination to assist her and Papa with the business, nor did I care a whit about the social aspects of post-war society. So what was to become of me? Neither of us had the slightest idea. Papa, however, came unexpectedly to my reluctant rescue.

My gallant efforts at assuming a countenance of normalcy had not fooled Papa in the slightest. I should have known they wouldn't, as he always knew the measure of our family and sometimes knew Solange and me better than we did ourselves. And certainly Solange and I thought we knew Papa better than he knew himself!

After dinner one evening in early March, Papa brought to the table a small bottle of fine port that he had "tucked away for just such a discussion," along with three small glasses that tinkled as he held them between the fingers of one hand. Before sitting back down, he poured us all a glass of the dark red wine.

My ears instantly picked up on his words. "What do you mean 'such a discussion'?"

He looked into his glass and watched the rich liquid swirl round and round before lifting the glass, inhaling, and at last taking a long sip. "A discussion about what is next for us all, *mes chers*. Now that the world has tilted on its axis but appears to have remained in orbit, we too must take a look at where we have landed after all the chaos. I, for one, am ready for some changes, and I want to hear from you both as to what you want to do, to be, and to become now that we are all here together. Let us spend some time in the contemplation of possibility." Papa relaxed back into his chair and took another drink, savoring the port and swallowing slowly.

Solange and I were sitting next to one another kitty-corner at the table from Papa, and as we looked at each other and before either of us said a word, Papa spoke again. And his words continued to surprise us.

"I have a few thoughts. Ideas, really, and options, more or less. I have worked for as long as I have memories. Life has been generous and rewarded our family with good health, a fine education for you both, warm friends, a secure home, and, most importantly, one another. Nothing is more valuable to me than the two of you. For better or worse, these last years of war and turmoil have resulted in affording us a future secured with monies invested and saved that will outlast us all. We can now contemplate what we could not have thought about during the chaos, when the possibility of no future was a reality. But all that is over. Behind us now. And time has come to make some practical plans." Papa smiled and conveyed to us, with a gesture of his hand, an invitation to speak.

Solange took her first sip of port and then said, "Papa, I am so relieved that this not a discussion regarding bad news such as financial ruin or reports of any ill health. You are fine in both areas?"

"*Oui oui!* And what is left of my life, our lives, I want to know we will spend in relative safety and fulfilling what have been plans and opportunities always promised somewhere in the future."

"And what do you mean by plans, Papa?" I asked.

He turned his eyes first to me and then Solange. "Do you remember each time I left to go to sea how you both plagued me with urgent requests to take you along? You must remember, for it has been all of your lives."

"Yes, of course," Solange said with a laugh, "and I still want to go each time you leave."

"And that is where the opportunity lies, *mes chers*!" Papa almost rose out of his seat with excitement. "We must give ourselves permission to visit in our minds where it is and what it is we would most like to experience and then make it reality. I know my voyages have taken me to places you both studied diligently in your books. I could only send or bring you trinkets home that might lend you some sense of what those places meant for me. But now we can go! Travel together to wherever it is we would like to spend time. Should either or both of you want to come with me, I would most definitely like to go to America."

Papa paused and took a sip of port. "I don't believe I have ever shared with you stories of my younger brother, Antoine?" he asked.

"No, Papa . . . ," Solange said as I met her look of consternation. "I'm quite certain you never mentioned you *had* a brother. Why have you not told us this before?"

"It is a long story and one my family regarded as a blight on our name. But Antoine and I are all that remains of us Chagalls, and although he left France twenty-five years ago, we have stayed in communication. Shortly after he married, he abandoned his young wife. Our family on both sides disowned him, and for reasons I have never fully inquired into, he fled to New York City. He has done well in commerce too, and now that I am relinquishing my business here, I am most interested in investing in Antoine's burgeoning enterprise in America. He wishes to expand, but I only want to invest and reap the financial rewards. I do not intend to become in any way involved with the running of another business."

Papa, always the pragmatist, took a deep breath and continued, "Placing our monies outside of Europe at this time and investing in the future growth in America seems wise. We will go to war again; this last conflict merely dampened the flame to embers. I have every intention of making a safe haven apart from any future conflict that will most likely tear apart the fabric of our culture to an even greater extent than what we can possibly imagine." Papa sat back in his chair, pursed his lips, raised his eyebrows, and drained the last of his fine port.

Glancing at Solange, I could feel her body almost shiver in anticipation of her lifelong dream of travel becoming reality. And then her body stilled as she quickly looked over at me. She well knew that traveling for travel's sake was not anything I aspired toward at this juncture in my life and that I would not find Papa's proposal appealing. But I remained quiet, thinking how I would possibly fit into these plans.

Papa saw this flash of understanding between Solange and me. And, of course, he was prepared for this as well.

"And you, my Marie. My brave warrior, my artist, my daughter with her mother's soul. I know these dreams of far travels are not now your own. Your future is yours to do with what you will. This house will be here, and you can remain here in Marseille, working as you might want . . . or not. But you have another option, a gift that has been long in coming, awaiting your arrival at a place where it would be received for what it was intended—a gift perhaps of refuge, peace, and new beginnings." He smiled and reached over, placing his warm hands upon mine.

"What are you talking about, Papa? What do you mean a gift?" I spoke quietly with caution and curiosity, wanting him to quickly tell it all.

"Your mother, Marie. She left for you her family's summer home. It is north, along the River Meuse, south of Verdun. I cannot know your feelings regarding anything that might lie in the North, with your having been through so much there. What I do know is that the house is standing in one piece, is in good repair, and sits directly across from the riverbank. There are no amenities—no running water or electricity—but my man who took a look in the past month assures me the stoves on both floors are in good condition, as is the one in the kitchen. The pump works well and the house stands much as it has for the last fifty years. This house in Meuse is where your *grand-maman* would take your maman and her brother for most of the summer, every year of their childhood. Your own maman, my dear Edith, told me countless stories of the summers she spent there in what she referred to as 'perfect bliss.'"

Papa's face relaxed, and with the soft voice of memory, he said, "After we married, your great-grand-maman gave the house to your maman as a wedding present. She and I visited it just once, shortly after our wedding and before you were born. Over these many years, from time to time, I have had someone look at it, and each time it was reported to be in good condition. I did not know how it would be found after the war, but to my amazement it has apparently not suffered any damage.

I sat there unmoving, staring intently across the table at Papa and wondering what to make of it all. His words I heard but could not begin to fathom their meaning, or what it was he expected me to do with what he had just imparted.

"I have a house, you say, Papa? A house on the River Meuse?"

"Yes, dear. And it is waiting for you whenever you might decide to pay it a visit. I am not suggesting that you go there any time soon, but as we begin to explore our possibilities, it seems appropriate to let you know of its existence. It may come to mean nothing to you, or you may become curious and want to see what your maman bequeathed to you."

He stopped there and quietly looked in my eyes. "But Marie, if you do make the decision to go to Meuse, you will do so with your mother's Gentile name as your own. You will be Marie Durant only. Chagall will need to remain in your past as you look to your future. The future of anyone named Chagall with any link to Judaism may come under suspicion. This war has stirred sentiments of deep-seated animosities and fear. When conflict comes again, and it will, it will do so fueled by intense revenge and obsession. Germany will not long suffer defeat, and when it moves again, we will have moved on."

Papa rose from his chair, saying, "There is a great deal for us each to think about. Let us sleep soundly and talk again in a few days when I return from what will be my last business venture. I have one more bottle of port to share with my daughters as we make our plans." He came round the table, kissed us each gently on both cheeks, and retired upstairs.

Solange looked at me and giggled. Actually giggled. A sound that was so infrequent and so joyful that I found myself laughing at her lightness. Obviously, a great weight had been removed from her. We both erupted into overlapping sentences acknowledging how happy we were to know that Papa was at last ready to retire from his affairs. I knew she too would relish shedding the burden of business.

I spoke the next words hoping they would relinquish her from any responsibility to me that might cause Papa and her to delay any plans for their adventures. "I may travel as well but only as far as Meuse, to at least see where my maman spent so much of her life. I might find something of mine there, you never know." I was silent for a moment. "Did you know about the house, Solange?" I asked in a near whisper.

She shook her head. "No, Papa has never breathed a word of it to me. I do not think it was an easy gift for him to deliver, knowing it might take you away from us again. But what he says is true: now is the time for you to know and make your own decisions." She rose in mid-yawn, kissed me good night, and went up to bed.

I remained at the table for quite some time trying to grab hold and make some sense of all the emotions vying for acknowledgement. My maman. I felt she was reaching out to me. Still caring for me, knowing that even now I would sense her watchfulness. The River Meuse. I did not know it, had not seen it during any of the time I spent in the North. It would be new to me and yet, knowing my mother had been so long in that place, might it also feel familiar? An unexpected gift from my own maman. The reassuring words I just spoke to Solange for her benefit might be truer than I knew. As Papa said, we needed time to spend in the contemplation of possibility. I toasted Maman and drained the last of the port from my glass.

CHAPTER 7

TO MEUSE, MAY 1920

During the time Papa was off on his last business venture, Solange and I spent almost all of our time discussing what he had shared. He departed the day after our talk, leaving so much unexplained but with the express instruction that we continue thinking about our options. Solange moved forward with complete confidence in their plans to travel, making tentative arrangements for them to visit first Spain and then on to Portugal, leaving sometime in May. She queried me daily as to what I thought might be my own plans: Would I be going with them, staying in Marseille, or was traveling to Meuse even an option? I would respond that I was continuing to think about it all.

"There is no hurry, Marie. No need to rush into anything you are not sure you want to do," she would say daily as well.

But I knew there was a sense of urgency. And I knew that I would not be traveling with them. The most reasonable option would be to remain in Marseille, at least for a short while, as I continued to ponder the possibility of a visit to Meuse. It was extremely difficult to think about the energy it would take to do anything at all other than sit in my chair in my painting studio. But I had to come to some decision, as I was sure Papa and Solange would not leave until they felt I was of a clear mind.

How in the world could Papa offer me such a "gift" that I was in no way ready to receive? Before he left that morning, he whispered in my ear, "Have courage!" I was afraid I was going to let him down. I had had courage once but thought I surely must have used up my allotment for life. How do you dredge up courage or even the appearance of courage where there is only a deep well of oblivion?

I began taking long walks alone down along the harbor. The days were becoming warm and the breeze off the sea was welcoming. I would stand at the edge of the water and close my eyes, envisioning the great sea wind moving through my mind and body, repairing scars and clearing out remnants of residual pain. Could a cleansing wind make enough room for the courage to do what I longed to do? To be brave once more and return to the North in anticipation that I might find there pieces of me that could make me whole? The truth was that when I left Marseille I was a seventeen-year-old girl wishing for independence and adventure. And here I was again, thinking of leaving but this time in search of meaning and peace. In that span of six years, so much had occurred, and I felt in many ways much older than my twenty-three years. Could I dare hope that in those years away I had developed reasoning mature enough to make a wise decision? But Papa wasn't asking me to be wise; he was asking me to be courageous. I thought there may be a great difference between the two.

By mid-April, Papa and Solange were packing trunks, their travel arrangements in place. They were leaving in two weeks for Spain with no plans other than to visit Portugal at some point and then continue to America. Regardless of my decision to stay or go north, we would keep the house in Marseille. Papa had made arrangements with our solicitor, and should I leave, the house would be looked after. In the midst of their packing and planning, Papa informed us that he had asked this same solicitor to update his will, stating the house, his holdings, and investments were to be left equally between Solange and me. Neither Solange nor I wanted to hear any of this, for it was extremely unsettling. Why was Papa thinking it necessary to have all this in place before they left? He also gave me a large envelope containing what he called my "new papers." With these, I felt he was assuming I had made the decision to venture to Meuse—that I had made the decision to become Marie Durant.

And thus, not knowing if it was Papa's silent prompting or my own true decision, I began packing my belongings as well. But, where Solange had several trunks, I packed only one. From my time at the front, I had learned that I needed very little in life and desired even less. I still had not spoken my intentions out loud, but my actions of sorting and packing implied my decision to travel north. Papa and Solange were bustling with eagerness to begin their adventures, and I too allowed myself some feeling of anticipation. And so I called this feeling courage. I would make it suffice.

The day before Papa and Solange were to take the train to Spain, they saw me, my single trunk, and one large tapestried bag off at the train station. I felt harried and prodded as they rushed me onto the platform, worried I might miss my train. Solange had tucked bills of money Papa insisted I take with me in small muslin bags, sewn them closed, and placed one by way of a belt round my waist beneath my dress and another on a heavy string round my neck. I was to wire Papa to send more money as needed. I did not count what monies went into those cloth bags but knew they would be more than sufficient to get me to Verdun and then on to the house in Meuse.

Solange's eyes streaming with tears and Papa's face holding tight against his own uncertainty, as they waved goodbye from the platform, left me feeling totally bereft. They were sending me away. I reasoned I had no other option than to leave. I did not want to go with them, but I could not stay behind. And there I was, steaming back on those rails to the source of my despair. Why did Papa not travel with me? He told me that when I arrived at the station in Verdun a burly middle-aged man named Bernard would be there to meet and assist me. But why did my own papa not deliver me to where he wanted me to go? I felt unloved, completely alone, and at that moment I could not have cared less what happened to me. I was being abandoned by the only people I loved.

I slept much of the journey north, arriving at the station in Verdun in the early morning two days later. True to his word, I was met on the platform by the burly man.

"Mademoiselle Durant? You can call me Bernard." His manner was overtly brusque, letting me know that friendly conversation was not required or invited. Papa said he had sent a wire instructing this man to take me to those establishments and shops in which I could procure an assortment of whatever I deemed "necessary for a comfortable visit."

With palpable reluctance, the large man drove me from the station to what shops in Verdun had survived the war as I assured him I needed little else than food.

"Mademoiselle, I know this house. It is empty and has not been lived in for many years. How are you to cook and what do you plan to sleep on?"

I acquiesced, and among several vendors I purchased a single mattress, bedding, two kerosene lamps, oil, matches, a few pots, dishes, and cutlery. Between what I had assembled and his own judgment regarding what he considered necessities, Bernard continued to add to the burgeoning pile of items stacked high on the shopkeepers' counters. I paid the goods little attention. While I handed over what seemed exorbitant amounts in payment, I paused to wonder why this stranger would even care what I purchased or did not. Then I realized that not only had Papa sent him instructions to pick up and deliver me to my destination, he had most likely also sent a list of what this man Bernard was to make sure I purchased to make my visit "comfortable."

Moving back and forth across town from shop to shop, we loaded the items into his truck, one purchase after the other, including two baskets of foodstuffs. It was obvious that after nearly three hours' time my escort was as tired of this tedious chore as I was, and I made the decision we had what was "necessary." What we hadn't found, I wouldn't need. After tying it all down with rope laid back and forth across the overflowing bed of his rattlebang vehicle, we began the drive south. Papa had shown me on a map where the house was approximately located. I took the map out of my bag and showed my escort where I thought it was we were going.

"I told you, I know the house. Checked it out myself as your father instructed me to," he said sharply, keeping his eyes straight ahead on the road. He looked as wornout and weary as his noisy truck sounded. I thought it likely he must not take any better care of himself than he did of his belongings.

I sat back, resigned to an unknown fate, keeping my eyes steeled on the map in front of me and trying not to look around at the ruin across the landscape. Evidence of the reality of my previous experience here. Recovery and rebuilding would take many years. In Verdun, the town we had just left, people were bustling with what appeared to be endless energy, continuing to reassemble their community and homes and put their lives back together. Watching them filled me with a sad weariness. I was not sorry to drive away south toward the country.

We drove for a good half hour. Every few minutes or so I thought the truck's horrible clangs and backfires would result in being stranded with this cantankerous man. Looking over at my driver, I watched him remove a dented silver container from his shirt pocket. He opened the tin of tobacco without taking his eyes from the road and wedged a large wad of the black strands up into his gums. What didn't make it into his mouth lay peppered across his shirtfront. Yes, Papa had abandoned me to unwelcoming strangers and a wasteland in every sense of the word.

The farther we drove south and east toward the river, the more I began to see open fields of land that appeared undisturbed from the last years of carnage. Along this stretch the Meuse would run wide for a bit and then narrow, with poplar trees scattered along its banks. As I began to settle into the winding of the river as we followed it, Bernard told me we were almost there.

After another ten minutes passed, he pulled the truck to a stop beside six worn, stone steps. They were set into a gentle incline bordered on each side by budding lavender leading to a stone front porch of a house.

My house.

I looked up at the house trying to take it in, but the sound of the river competed for my attention. It was easier to keep my eyes toward the river's flow than turn round to this empty structure.

"And here we are, Mademoiselle. I have the key to give you. We'll unload your goods and I'll be on my way." It was dusk by the time we hauled everything inside, depositing all the items on the floor of a large room just inside the front door.

"Should you need me, just ask anyone in town." With a swift, fluid motion, he extended his fisted hand toward me, and as I reached out to meet it, he dropped a large silver house key into my open palm. It was cold and heavy. He then bid me adieu and spun around, as if in a great hurry to get away. His motor started with a loud bang and off he drove, leaving me alone and exhausted.

The light was almost gone as I pushed my trunk to one corner of the front room, dragged the mattress up against the wall under the front window, and left everything else in heaping piles against the opposite walls. I pulled a blanket from one of the piles, lay down, tucked myself in, and fell immediately into sleep. My last thought was one of relief—relief that I was alone and had no one to make an effort for. Not Papa, not Solange, not acquaintances, and certainly not for Bernard. It was enough of an effort to just be with myself, and I would begin to deal with me tomorrow.

CHAPTER 8

CLEANING THE ROOMS, AUGUST 1920

As I sat outside on the front steps with only an old shawl wrapped round me, I thought how the chill was unexpected for such a late summer's day. I realized my only comparison of what might be typical or not of August weather was the hot and windy summer days of Marseille, far south on the Mediterranean Sea.

I knew the cold could come quickly here, which meant I would soon have to consider securing winter wood for the house stoves. As I scanned all around, I saw few trees other than the river's poplars standing in such a straight line along the bank. Surely there were trees somewhere nearby that could provide an ample supply of wood, I thought, straining to look farther in the distance. Bringing my thoughts back to today, the flowing fields of late-blooming lavender, and the constant humming from the throngs of bees all around me, I vowed to enjoy the last of the summer.

When I arrived in May, the days were just beginning to warm, and the relief in finding myself alone was so great and the returning despair so numbing, I was not aware of any sensations of cold or warmth, day or night. Now, sitting here in this bright light, I felt just the beginnings of my own thaw.

Disturbing these tranquil thoughts, I heard the peddler, Henri, approaching from the south before I caught sight of his donkey and wagon. He had stopped by every week or so since my arrival. One of my first purchases from him had been six young laying hens, and I had been exchanging their large brown eggs with him for bread and cheese since. As was our usual conversation, we politely discussed the weather and what I needed to purchase.

Since I had no means of transportation to travel to town, he also brought my mail, which often included welcome letters from Solange and Papa. Along with stories of their travels, the envelopes included money and occasionally a box with a thoughtful gift, such as handkerchiefs, teas, a piece of jewelry, or a book, and sometimes a small painting or sculpture. It reminded me of when Papa would send us treasures from exotic places, and now Solange was doing the same. I took to displaying the items she sent, arranging them by arrival on a folded blanket on the floor of my front room. These tokens of familial love were the sole sparks of color and whimsy within my world. I never wore the jewelry and used little of the money. The money I did spend was to purchase items from Henri, essentials I needed to sustain my life here. The larger amounts of money from Papa that Solange had sewn into the small muslin bags remained in their cases, tucked into the back of an empty kitchen drawer.

With her almost-weekly letters and gifts, Solange always sent a blank piece of paper and an envelope addressed to where she and Papa were planning to remain for the next few weeks. I knew she was desperate for news of me, news that I was indeed in improving health and that I felt safe. She never inquired about my returning to the house in Marseille nor did she suggest I join her and Papa, and for that I was grateful. I had written them twice each month in the three since my arrival in Meuse. With each letter I assured Solange I was intact, felt I had made a wise decision to visit this place, thanked them for the money or the gift, and told her to be sure to relay to Papa my love and gratitude. I also requested that a smaller portion of money be sent to me the next time or even no money at all until the first of the year, as I had more than enough to keep me until then.

My days moved quietly and with complete predictability, one into the other, and there was little to write that a reader might find of interest. Other than expressing my gratitude and my love and the state of my hens, there was little else to say. I realized it was solace for them just to know I felt secure in this place

I had reluctantly chosen. It had now become my haven and that, at least, I was always able to convey with no hesitation.

As Henri and his donkey approached, I stood and with a wave of my hand and a shake of my head indicated I needed nothing, and he could continue on his route without stopping. As I turned back toward the house, he waved his hand above his head and called, "Wait, Mademoiselle! I have news for you!"

I could not imagine what it was he had to tell me but stayed put until he came along in front of my steps. Did he have another box or letter perhaps?

"Good day, Mademoiselle! Are you enjoying this cool afternoon?"

"Yes," I said, quietly adding that it seemed early for such a fall-like day. It passed through my mind to ask him where I might find wood but he continued on before I had the chance.

"Mademoiselle, thank you for receiving me this morning. Do you know of the convent just an hour or so north of here?"

I shook my head with a soft, "No."

"After the conflict, the Sisters at the convent gave much-needed care to men too sick to immediately return home to their families. They are a small order and can only house and care for no more than five or six of our brave soldiers at a time. These men have wounds to the flesh as well as grave wounds to the spirit, which, as I'm sure you can understand, are often more difficult to heal. The Sisters believe that with time and tending these wounded men will repair sufficiently to travel home, but they simply don't have room to house all who need care. That is why I wanted to speak with you today, Mademoiselle. You have empty rooms here, no? You could care for perhaps three of these brave men of ours, no?"

As he finished this long soliloquy, the most words I had heard from another person in my several months here, I crossed my arms and just stared at him. Surely I had not understood his questions, I thought. He remained still, head cocked to one side, and I realized I had heard correctly.

"No," I said in a whisper caught in my throat. I was surprised at how feeble it sounded, as I had attempted to yell my response as loudly and emphatically as possible. I could barely care for my own basic needs! I had nothing to offer these men. I told him again, with more voice this time. "No, no, Monsieur, I am not under any circumstances able to accommodate wounded soldiers."

"It is only three men, Mademoiselle. Men very young and completely alone. The Sisters say they do not talk, do not yet walk, and make no demands. They would need only to stay in their beds. . . . And you have bedrooms, no?"

I had ventured to the upstairs of the house perhaps a handful of times, not even curious to open the doors to what I supposed were bedrooms. No need to know what was above me; I was perfectly happy existing only in the space below. Apart from the table and bench in the kitchen and my mattress and trunk, there was no other furniture on the ground floor, and I had no recollection of any furniture on the landing above.

"No, no, no!" I told him again. "This would not be possible. There is nothing I can do."

"Please, Mademoiselle. The good Sisters need your help, as do these young men. They assured me that provisions would be supplied to assist in providing care, including wood for the coming winter. The men will need warmth, as will you, Mademoiselle."

How could he possibly know of my concern for acquiring wood for the winter? Was this a conjured scheme to ensure my acquiescence to this outrageous plan? Again and again, I told him no. It was unthinkable!

"Mademoiselle, the good Sisters asked me to help find a place for these three fragile souls. I told them of your large home and that I would merely ask. I will let them know of your consideration."

Consideration? It was not consideration but adamant refusal! Thinking that was the end of the matter and with a fearful suspicion I would not entertain, I quickly turned my back on Henri, this curious, meddling, persistent peddler, and retreated back into my house.

Shaking and barely able to reach the kitchen's darkness, I fell onto the seat of the wooden bench and laid my head on the table to subdue the rising nausea. I could not look into eyes of misery again, could not give any touch of comfort, for it would not matter in the least and they would die regardless. No, I had nothing to give, and the very thought of the attempt sent fear throughout my body. I swallowed down the rising bile in my throat as I struggled to shut away from memory the long-suppressed visions assaulting my senses.

Who were these young men once full of passion and eager to begin the battle? Battle for what? For what had they truly fought? I knew these men. Knew they believed zeal and a demand for justice would guarantee that the righteous would be victorious. Knew we all believed that those sacrificed millions who moved to defend and protect us from evil would surely be surrounded by cloaks of impenetrable goodness, and return home whole and healthy to heal our parched lands.

Was the victory worth the sacrifice of the scores upon scores of those lost to battle? Lost forever was a generation upon whom we had laid our destiny: our fathers, sons, brothers, husbands, our mothers, wives, sisters, and countless friends. We were left with our land free of evil but with losses so wretched we could not savor the victory.

Later that day, once I had gathered my senses, I ascended the creaking stairs, dust motes floating in rays of light leading the way upward. The top of the staircase opened onto a broad L-shaped landing, which was wider to my left, to the north. Around the landing were what I assumed to be three bedrooms. The doors were closed and the rooms waiting: a large one in the northwest corner and two smaller ones on the other side of the landing.

Straight before me at the top of the stairs was a grand window framed in decorative lead with views long-looking to the west, over the land—my land. Not for the first time, I was caught amazed that this beautiful land was truly mine. Nineteen hectares, Papa had told me. The view was captivating. Today, I wanted to move through this window and fly across the blue waves of lavender before me.

How long I stood looking west from this window I do not know. I felt a settling of spirit, gained a grounding, and turned to my left. I walked from the top of the stairs across the wide-plank wood floors of the landing, which seemed a cozy common area where people might have sat round the stove. This second-floor wood stove was settled onto a slate slab identical to the one on the first floor, directly below it, with a large pipe of metal extending through both of them, on up and out the ceiling. Both stoves were square, heavy cast iron, simple in design and without ornament, with a locking handle on the glass-fronted doors. They had been cleaned thoroughly some time before my arrival. Whoever had left this house however long ago left nothing behind—not even ashes in a stove to indicate life had ever been lived here.

I looked at the closed bedroom doors one by one. Had my mother also walked the empty house closing these same doors before she left that last time? I felt a strong sense of her, of a mother I never knew but knew had loved me. How long and with whom had she lived here? Without realizing, I had moved to the door of the closest bedroom, the one in the northwest corner, and I found my hand on the knob, turning it. I slowly pushed open the door and stepped just inside. Did I imagine the air rushing around me, escaping as an exhalation after having been cooped inside for so long? Holding its breath until someone returned to breathe life into this empty house again?

There were windows, large closed windows, on the east and west walls of the room. A large bed frame of light-colored wood, bare of mattress, was pushed up tight against the wall, its footboard ending just at the edge of the west-facing window, allowing some view out. A matching mid-height dresser, three drawers high resting on wide, curved legs, stood against the wall beside the bed, its surface empty except for a layer of dust. To my immediate left were a small round table and two chairs, nicked and worn with use. The furniture was the same golden color as the planks of the flooring, making them seem parts of the whole, as though they had grown up from the roots of the floor. The presence of furniture caught me by surprise. I had not expected any evidence of people's daily lives. But here I faced proof that my other family had been real, had lived here in this house. I felt a deep longing for these people of mine whom I had never known.

At that moment, the sun decided to emerge from behind a cloud. The thin layer of dust I had disturbed upon my entrance danced in the air, appearing alive and moving in the afternoon light pouring in from the west window. I looked round the space once more and then turned and left the room, which I now thought of as "the first bedroom."

Now that one room was exposed, I could move to the other two, perhaps better prepared to meet an unknown past. I proceeded across the landing and entered the bedroom in the southwest corner. Other than one bed frame of the same light wood in the corner by the southwest-facing window, this room was empty. This became "the second bedroom." With the exception of dust made visible in the sunlight from the windows, the third bedroom in the southeast corner was entirely bare.

This was weary work, opening what had long been void and empty. The fear that I might find the rooms filled with personal items from my family was abating. Finding only the few pieces of furniture, bed frames, and nothing more was a welcome relief. Emptiness was familiar and required nothing of me.

That evening, just as the sun began its descent for the day, I walked up the stairs again and from the landing window admired the lavender in full, vibrant bloom flowing to the horizon. My magic carpet I could jump onto from this window. In another few weeks it would begin its late-summer fade.

Early the next day found me watching the morning light through that same window, the purple-blue hues coming awake in the fields. With the sun came a breeze like life moving across the land, waves upon waves of a lavender sea. I could not deny the joy I felt each time I looked through those panes. My breath caught as the light found and held all of me through that window.

Feeling a sense of mounting obligation to do justice to this house, to offer what gratitude I could for this gift of mine, I began to clean. Not because I was entertaining any thought whatsoever of occupants but rather because I wanted my entire house in respectable condition, top to bottom. Thus with mop, rags, and a steaming bucket of suds in hand, I climbed the stairs and filled my soul with whatever it could store from the dawn's light and began to scrub each room in the order I had assigned them. The first bedroom, then the second and third. The landing was scoured last, beginning with the stove now freed of webs and dust.

While I could not empty my soul of all that made it feel scarred, it felt good to remove from this second floor all that had lain dormant in the dusty remains of a past. And the windows, all the windows up there, especially my large window on the landing, were free to once again admit the light and the shadows. With the landing and bedrooms now damp and smelling of wet wood from the scrubbing, I made my way on hands and knees, scouring one step at a time down the stairs. Standing at the bottom, out of breath, my long-unused muscles let me know they were ready for a rest. Afternoon had settled in. The time had passed unawares, as I had entertained no other thoughts than ridding every upstairs space of dust and cobwebs. As I stood there looking up at my work and feeling a sense of great accomplishment, my stomach rumbled loudly. I was hungry. Really hungry! Something I had not felt in such a long time.

A week had now passed since I last saw Henri, and I was expecting his return any day. I was not looking forward to his additional pleas, his harping about my caring for the wounded. While, yes, the bedrooms were clean, I had done so for me and not in any anticipation of them being filled with damaged souls. Besides, there were only two bed frames and no mattresses.

Sure enough, Henri arrived the next day and asked how this day found me. I saw his eyes take in my rough, red hands, for I had continued my manic cleaning to include scrubbing thoroughly all the downstairs as I had not done before, especially the forlorn kitchen with its dust-layered shelves and drawers and wood-burning cooking stove sprinkled with rodent droppings, which alone took me hours. All the windows upstairs and down now glistened, allowing in light through every pane. The lingering smell of the vinegar I used to make my windows shine remained in the house as well as on my hands. I loved coming in from outside to be greeted by that pungent scent.

"You have been working hard, no, Mademoiselle?"

Did he miss nothing, this prying man?

"Yes," I said quickly and went on with a harried explanation. "I have been cleaning. Cleaning my house because it was about time I completed the long-overdue task. However, the rooms remain entirely unsuitable for residents. There is a complete lack of furniture, two bed frames only and no mattresses at all, not to mention no linens, bedding, or food stores, and all else that would be needed to provide adequate accommodations for nursing care." I paused to take a breath I could not quite catch and hurried on, "It is not at all possible to tend ones so needy with nothing more than empty rooms! Surely the Sisters understand these men need to be sent somewhere more suitable. Caring for them here is not a responsibility I can even remotely consider. This is an outrageous idea and not to be entertained in any way!" Out of breath again, I held my tightly fisted hands against my sides and glared, with as firm a face as I could muster, forcefully into Henri's eyes.

"But empty rooms are exactly what is needed! There are no obstacles here, Mademoiselle! Your list of needed items is but a small consideration that can be easily accomplished. I am on my way north now and feel certain I can locate what you require to make 'adequate accommodations.'

"I will return in a week's time, Mademoiselle, for the Sisters say to tell you the men will be arriving in fewer than ten days. We will need to work quickly, but with the cleaning done, all we need are another bed frame and mattresses."

Filled with frustration, I stomped my foot and shouted, "Henri, listen to me! That is not all that is needed! How can you possibly secure all that is needed? Mattresses, linens, towels, soaps, bedpans, a hanging line, pots, pans, food, and medical supplies? And probably twenty other things I haven't even thought of."

"Oui, oui. Everything will be found," he said calmly, the absurdity of the situation seemingly not penetrating his senses. "Perhaps not all at once," he went on, "but we will find what you need to begin, and you need only to begin, Mademoiselle. The Sisters will provide at least one change of bed linens, clothes, and other provisions, including a large supply of winter wood, of course."

"Henri, have you even seen these men?" I demanded to know.

"No. But what would it matter? What is most important is that you are well and ready to tend them and nothing more."

Mon Dieu! What was happening? Shaking and nauseated once more, I quickly passed Henri my overflowing basket of eggs. He in turn extended a basket with its contents wrapped in white linen, which I hastily grabbed from his hands with a grunt of dismissal. I nearly dropped it, as its heavy weight was unexpected. I could not meet his eyes. I turned and quickly retreated into my house. This time I did not seek the dark kitchen, instead hurrying up the stairs to my clean window on the landing. I folded to the floor and held my pounding head in my shaking hands. Slowly, the fear and astonishment at what was about to begin faded as I realized I smelled a familiar fragrance that caused my mouth to water. Was I always hungry these days?

Upon unfolding the white linen and peering into the basket, I found bread, cheese, and two oranges—large, bright-colored orbs whose fragrance had caused me to pause in my worry. I sat in an incandescent pool of bright light that had warmed the wood of the landing floor and, using the linen from the basket as my spread cloth, laid out the store of food. I pulled apart the bread, tore a chunk of cheese to place atop it, and peeled an orange, eating it quickly while licking the sweet juice dripping from my fingers, and thought there was nothing to even be concerned about. Henri would never find everything that was needed to allow me to care adequately for these soldiers and, truth be told, I thought him smart enough to know that this idea was both foolish and flawed. And all else he might be, I did not think him a fool.

CHAPTER 9

THE BOYS ARRIVE, SEPTEMBER 1920

H enri did not return in seven days but nine. During that time, restlessness and anxiety found me endlessly pacing—outside, inside, upstairs and downstairs, again and again. No daily walks to the river, though, as I didn't want to miss hearing his approach.

That ninth day, he arrived mid-morning, traveling from the north. As I looked down the road, I saw pieces of wood strapped to the top of his wagon and long, stuffed packs wobbling left and right across his donkey's back with each swaying step. My heart fell realizing that his haul was to be delivered at my doorstep. Where would he ever have found all this? Who had given him these supplies and who paid the cost? These questions would come to my mind time and again over the next many months, but they never found way to my lips, and Henri never volunteered answers.

I prepared harsh words for him as I marched down the steps, but as he got nearer, I realized his wasn't the victorious face of someone succeeding in his mission. Instead, I saw deep lines of fatigue framing his eyes, dreading rejection. He stopped the wagon and sat stone-still upon its seat. As I looked up at him, standing still myself, we took measure of one another. I can only imagine what my countenance reflected. Surely he saw my expression change from determined steadfastness to one of confused empathy.

He jumped down from the wagon's seat with a heavy grunt and turned to face me. He was slightly taller than me, but we were close enough in height that we were near equal. He was expecting my refusal but hoping for acknowledgement that what he brought in offering would be accepted. I found that I too was waiting for my own acknowledgement. I realized I had days ago acquiesced to this scheme, but he could not know that. With a nod of my head indicating hesitant willingness, I said, "Let's see what you have brought."

He began to unload the rails of a wooden bed frame, but before he could lay the first piece to the ground, I lifted one end and together we carried it into the house and up the stairs. The spans of wood felt too light to support a body, but perhaps the whole would be more substantial than each piece separately. The wood was dark, old, and highly polished—obviously a fine piece at one time. I wondered and quickly decided that, most likely, Henri had cleaned and polished it hoping I might find it suitable. Once we had all the pieces in the second bedroom we fit it together easily. I wanted two of the men to share this room, keeping the third for storage and supplies that I would need close by to avoid running up and down the stairs. Even as we carried the furniture into place I continually acknowledged that, indeed, I had given this much thought and had the spaces carefully planned out and allotted. Now with two bed frames in the room, we moved the headboards against the west wall with enough room between for a table, which Henri carted up from the wagon.

Next, we unloaded unwieldy stacks of linens, each of us carrying up a heavy pile and setting it on the floor beneath the window. Going back for a second load, we left the landing strewn with unmatched, worn fabrics of differing weights in shades of browns and beiges. The blandness had an unintended calming effect on me and aroused no turmoil; the piles of cloth were harmlessly unintimidating. Henri assured me there were two changes of linens for each bed plus clothes, towels, washcloths, blankets, and other assorted items that might be needed. We then struggled for the next hour to haul upstairs and onto the bed frames three ungainly mattresses in various states of repair.

The wagon empty of furniture, Henri took the liberty to look about the landing and then move to each of the bedrooms and stand, as I had done at first, just in the doorways. His eyes traveled over the clean expanse of the rooms.

"Windows in each room. Morning and afternoon sun good for healing. And this long landing will be a place for them to exercise, to stretch and walk about. Of course, not at first but in good time, no?"

When I asked, he told me the light-colored plank floors in all the house and the furniture in the first bedroom were made of beech wood. "Beech trees grow extensively in this part of France, and the mellow golden wood graces the homes of many."

All I thought as we headed back down those stairs was that this was as bad an idea as ever conjured by good people. Once outside, we stood by the wagon, each contemplating the days ahead.

"And I will also be needing a supply of food and kitchen staples. I have the money to pay for all else that is needed," I said. (Thank you, Papa.)

"Let's see what else I've got for you here," Henri replied, anticipating my needs, as always.

That day, I purchased from him soap, dry beans and flour, salt and sugar, and *saucisson*, a delicious dry cured sausage, and I insisted he take my money. Henri insisted I also needed yeast, as he assumed I would be baking bread, and handed me a wet, fragrant lump wrapped in a damp cloth.

From the depths of the wagon, he also pulled out a large wood-slatted crate. "And this," he added. "You can't do without this: salt pork, dried fish, potatoes, and onions!" Without waiting for any comment from me, he picked up the box and carried it to my front porch.

I stood holding the yeast, taking in its earthy scent, which sent memories wafting through my mind. It was all I allowed myself to think about.

Solange and I had spent much time in our sunny kitchen watching and chatting with Elise as she cooked and made bread. When Papa was away and Elise released for a week or two by Solange to visit her family, "at full pay, of course" she always assured her, we even tried to follow our beloved cook's recipes, including making our own bread, which was never quite up to Elise's.

While I was lost in my nostalgia, Henri had removed several more items from the wagon, which were now lying about me on the ground. He and his donkey had brought so much! And now he would be leaving again. Leaving me with all this, and I had no idea where to begin to sort it all out.

"Three days from now," he said, holding up three fingers. "I will return in three days with your men." He turned and climbed aboard his wagon.

My men? Three days?

"And with more provisions, of course, Mademoiselle Marie. The Sisters will send along what they also feel necessary for their care. Do not worry, for you will do them justice."

Henri's donkey turned at that moment of my doubt, looked into my eyes, and with a shake of his head let out a low bellow. He seemed to be telling me to have courage. Desperately needing something to hold on to, I walked over to this weathered, dusty, brown animal, flung my arms round his neck, and buried my head in his sun-warmed hide.

Three days. Three days. Who was I to dispense justice to anyone? These men were damaged. There would be no justice for them now or ever. And most certainly there was none in my power to bestow. With those thoughts, I reluctantly let go of Donkey and bid Henri adieu.

In three days, a wagon did come from the north. Not Henri's boxy, closed wagon but one open and flat. Wide enough for three men to lie side by side, I thought as it approached. Henri sat atop this first wagon pulled by a large brown horse. I assumed they belonged to the Sisters at the convent. Donkey followed along behind, pulling his usual load of his own wagon, again piled high with items strapped, tied, and hanging all across his back and sides.

They approached slowly. Were the men injured still of body and not just of mind, requiring that no jarring or running over ruts should occur? It seemed a long time after the battles for that to be the case. I waited on my steps next to the road, shading my eyes with my hand for a better view of what was to befall me.

"We need to get them inside. They are hot and moaning," Henri said as he jumped from his seat and hurried toward the back of the wagon and the waiting men.

I eased myself forward to look inside. The men lay head to foot, foot to head, beside one another. Young, very young. Two strawberry-blond and freckled, the other darker of hair. All medium height and severely emaciated. Their eyes were closed and they lay motionless, with only low moans emanating from them. From one or two or all of them? I could not tell but the sound was familiar to me. I heard it my sleep when I saw mounds of men sprawled in each other's blood and crooning a plea for death. So much of the time there was nothing, nothing to be done. My own moaning often merged with theirs, and still, some mornings I woke myself up with the sound. Would these men now wake me up as well? All of us waking together in a chorus of torment? As Henri began lifting the first man out of the wagon, the one of darker hair, I moved without hesitation to assist. Again, what else was there to do now?

Henri said the Sisters thought this man was named Laurent. He could walk just a little if assisted. With support from Henri on his left and me on his right, we managed to half-drag the weak man into the house and up the stairs to his assigned room. I gave him the first bedroom, the northwest room. Maybe he would soon be able to sit at the table to take his food. And then soon thereafter be able to leave.

After settling Laurent onto his bed, we returned to the others. Together Henri and I lifted one man at a time, rescuing their slack bodies from the hard bottom of the wagon. I gripped their ankles, thin as spindles, while Henri's hands supported them beneath their underarms, and we moved as quickly as possible to the house. With great care, we climbed the stairs and placed each man atop his own mattress in the second bedroom.

They were, the three of them, dressed in heavy wool pants and thin long-sleeved shirts. All torn, stained, and missing buttons. Battlefield leftovers, clean but scarred. An outer covering for what lay identical beneath.

I asked Henri if they had changes of clothing.

"There is one jacket and another pair or two of wool pants. The Sisters had nothing else to spare. It is fortunate they are all of one size, no? And there are gowns among the linens, I think."

I had made up the beds days ago and sorted the linens by placing them in separate piles of blankets, sheets, towels, and clothes on the floor of the third bedroom. There had been only three bed gowns, two pairs of pants, and one shirt. I emphatically told Henri that only loose-fitting clothes were to be brought to me, and thick linen pads for the beds had to be found. No wool garments. Only cotton or linen that could be washed and dried quickly.

Seeing my look of frustration, he immediately assured me he would take care of it. According to the Sisters, none of the men were able to use a chamber pot on their own and so often soiled themselves. Henri must have known something of what this care entailed.

"I understand the urgency, Mademoiselle Marie! Truly I do." I believed him and also believed he was glad to be the one securing the garments and not changing the beds.

"And a drying line, Henri. Did you bring a drying line?" I asked as we stood peering into the third bedroom at the meager sorted piles of bedding, towels, and clothes on the floor against one wall.

"Oui! And I have more soap. The drying line can be hung out back by the pump. I will see to it before I leave. And I also brought a large washtub and washboard. Your pump is situated well for the laundry, no?" My only hope for sustaining changes of clean, dry laundered items for each man was warm, dry days.

Checking on the men once again, we found them quiet, and I covered each with a thin blanket. For all appearances, they were sleeping peacefully. We moved quietly down the stairs and out to Henri's own wagon. He had unhitched Donkey, who was now standing in front of the flat open wagon as if ready to have his goods unloaded off his back.

And unload goods Henri did! The baskets and crates strapped to Donkey's sides were full of dried foods, fresh foods, breads, cheeses, oats, vegetables, and more flour. Even dried apples and honey from the convent, Henri said. Oh my! My kitchen shelves would be full for the first time.

Henri placed it all on the ground, and looking at this bounty, I wondered if these men high above me would even be able to eat. Surely any means of sustenance would need to be soft and moist and little at a time. I understood that Henri did not just bring these items for the men. They were offerings of atonement to me in exchange for what he and others perceived to be my good heart and capable nursing skills in caring for these soldiers.

Henri last brought forth another basket of gray-blue wicker, rectangular with handles woven into the sides. He lifted it gently by those handles and laid it on the drop-down back of his wagon. The basket was filled to overflowing with clean, white towels.

"Mademoiselle Marie, I did not forget you said some time ago you needed towels for yourself. Here are towels for your use alone and also a small token of gratitude."

He began to slowly pull the towels apart, seeming to prolong his own excitement with the hope that I might feel a sense of anticipation as well. Among the towels was a fine tea set of thin bone china. Henri carefully laid out each piece on the wagon lid: four delicate cups placed atop four matching saucers. The blue-flowered pattern was reminiscent of the tea service Solange and I had used all our years in Marseille. I was quite moved by this gift and even more by this man's thoughtfulness on my behalf.

Henri cleared his throat. "The kind woman who so generously provided this china set said she did so for the benefit of aiding in any way the recovery of your men. She could not, however, spare her sugar tongs, but as we have no sugar cubes, I told her all the better, no?"

Smiling at Henri's remarks, I wondered if the thick white towels were coerced from this woman's home as well. Four of them, as though they were additional pieces of the tea set. And there was also a tin of loose tea leaves. "China tea," Henri added as if an afterthought.

He quickly rewrapped the delicate china in the soft folds of the towels and placed it all into the basket. Presenting the basket to me with a slight bow and a soft adieu, he made as if to leave.

Sudden fear of abandonment assaulted me. "Henri, wait!" I said, stepping forward. "I need to know when you will return. What if I need something urgently for one of the men?"

"I'll return in three days." He smiled. "This time with wood!" He climbed into his seat, took up Donkey's reins, and departed.

Item by item, I carefully picked up and carried into the house what I knew were donations and contributions that Henri had collected from what I hoped were willing people. Two bed trays and a cracked but large and low chamber pot were among the array of goods. Now I had two, so this pot would belong to the men, and I would keep mine as my own. At times I had the feeling Henri most likely bewitched others to do his bidding, much as he had bewitched me. Hopefully he had not snatched this pot from beneath someone unawares!

I delivered the foodstuffs into the kitchen and spread it all out atop the table before arranging the items across my clean, empty shelves. All other various and assorted items I left on the floor in the sitting room. Where to put it all? I had no shelves other than the ones in the kitchen, and those were now full. No table in my dining room or armoires for storage either. I put it out of my mind, deciding I would sort it all later and move everything to do with the men to the third bedroom above.

It was now early evening and the men were still sleeping. As I checked on them, I was once again struck by their youth. Laurent looked the eldest of the three. Looking again at the two other men, boys really, I thought once more of how alike they were, with few features differing one from the other. Could they be brothers by blood as well as battle?

These men were known to me. They were my kin, my fellows from the trenches. I felt safe in their shared despair. Despair so entrenched in the soul it would be easy, so preferable, to die. I had been there with them. Knew the sights and smells and sounds they could not face. This sleep kept their minds locked safely away from the conscious reality of despair that awaited them. I felt a sudden rekindling of compassion at the sight of these skeletal boys. But no, it was not compassion. It was selfishness. A fake empathy. I had no other choice but to say yes to Henri and the Sisters' request to care for these boys. I was to be a parasite feeding on their anguish to keep me alive. Perhaps by saving them I could save myself as well.

CHAPTER 10

LAURENT, SEPTEMBER 1920 – JUNE 1921

Through fall and into November, Henri passed often on the road to and from Verdun, sometimes stopping and sometimes not. Busy with the boys (I could not bring myself to call these young injured souls men), I did not always see him as he traveled by my house. Evidence of his fleeting presence was found at least twice monthly, sometimes as often as every ten days, in the provisions he left on my front porch—food and clothes and linens for the boys. I always put a basket of eggs outside for him round the time I thought he might pass. Mingled among the more general supplies from Henri, I would also find a treat or an item I knew he felt might be appreciated or helpful. Two red apples, a square of dark chocolate, or perhaps a fragrant tea. Once, a new knife, sharp and long, and another time a new razor to shave their chins. I always imagined these as bribes, small treats to keep me from throwing up my hands and leaving the boys outside my door to cart away rather than my basket of brown eggs. But every surprise was appreciated and often caused me to smile, and yes, there was anticipation.

Henri's passings often felt clandestine. Did he not announce himself thinking perhaps it would interrupt my care of the boys and my constant washing, cooking, feeding, changing, and cleaning? Yes, it would have interrupted my day, and how welcomed it would have been! Someone to talk with, and not just to talk at, would have been appreciated. I sometimes felt as though Henri snuck off quietly to preclude any chance of my reneging on this commitment. Once again, I felt abandoned.

Of course, it's also possible Henri passed unannounced because he believed my daily routines and patterns of tending were rituals that aided my own healing and were therefore not to be disturbed. Not even for welcomed company. Indeed, I would have most likely complained bitterly and harangued Henri with protests and angst. It wasn't fair that all this care fell to me! And with no help from him! In my own fear and feelings of helplessness, I would not have recognized his gifts and provisions as proof of his watchfulness and affirmations regarding my own abilities. As my days were physically exhausting, there was little to no time for thoughts of self and even less for self-pity. I sunk into dreamless sleep each night, never waking myself again with noises from the past.

Some mornings I awoke more cheerful than others. On those days I would greet the boys with a hearty "Bonjour!" Other mornings I found myself struggling with self-doubt, as the passing days saw no discernible improvement in their condition.

Days were organized around feeding times, and I truly thought of them as feeding times and not mealtimes. Mealtimes were events shared round a table with others who actively participated in conversation and the passing and enjoyment of foods. Mealtimes conjured memories of dinners with Solange, Papa, and our frequent guests, their smiles of anticipation reflected brightly in the candles gracing the long, formal table.

Feeding times with the boys reminded me of feeding animals—initially reluctant animals at that. I prepared porridge with salt and sugar and cups of strong tea, carting it upstairs on trays before filling their mouths with spoonfuls of the warm mush.

The boys in the second bedroom, so similar in all ways, I thought of as "the brothers," and I always attended to them first. I would lay their food tray on the table and shake them gently, or sometimes not so gently, into a state of wakefulness so they were at least alert enough to accept the spoon into their almost-always drowsy mouths. Initially, they all needed their well-cooked, sodden oats delivered to them in this way. The breakfast of oatmeal never varied, and after a few weeks, they seldom refused to eat.

I would sometimes chatter about the food, the weather, asking did they sleep well, telling them the plan for the day, and all of this in the time it took for me to feed one and then the other as their bowls emptied and they swallowed their tea. Then, laying the bowls and cups aside, I would wash their faces and change their pants, leaving further ministrations until later in the morning.

Mornings and evenings were the busiest. During the first few weeks with me, they slept for most of every afternoon. Every other day I gave them full bed baths and changed their bed linens. On Mondays, they were shaved—"Monday shaves" as I told them. I moved from one boy's tending to the next throughout each day, and each day moved seamlessly into weeks.

Laurent I would feed and wash after the brothers. He appeared some years older than them and, unlike them, always seemed somewhat present. I sensed he could understand my words and had his own thoughts, yet he never spoke to me with anything other than his eyes. I would catch him surreptitiously watching me as I set his tray upon the table in his room or as I straightened his bed. I was never overly cheerful or chatty with him as I was with the brothers. We seemed, both of us, to require and appreciate an honesty about the situation. Laurent tolerated my assistance, and I sensed that he perhaps remembered something of what had occurred to bring him to this place. He often seemed so aware of his surroundings and yet restless and despondent. Could he see pain reflected in my eyes as I could in his own?

Laurent, after the first week of his arrival, began to flinch with each approach of my spoon, putting up his hand as though to deflect any more intrusion to his person. If he could lift his hand toward his mouth, could he not lift his own spoon? And he did. With hand over hand coaxing, he was soon feeding himself with no help from me other than encouragement to "eat it all."

As the weeks moved forward, Laurent's eyes remained pools of sorrow. Occasionally, I saw a reflection of defiance at my constant and sometimes forceful promptings to eat, walk, wash, and dress himself. He would succumb, I think, only to stop my ceaseless nagging to walk farther, eat more, put on his shirt, use the pot by himself, and on and on.

To my mind, his efforts toward self-care demonstrated he was healing and perhaps soon he would begin to talk and tell me the name of his family. I encouraged him to try and told him if he could, he would be reunited with them. His growing ability to meet his own needs allowed me more time to tend to the other young men who still remained little changed from when they arrived. While the brothers now spent their waking time with opened eyes, I did not believe they truly saw anything of their present surroundings or situation. They continued to cry out in the night during their sleep from dreams that were surely haunting. I spoke with them during their feedings and tending, and while they would reflexively open their mouths as the spoon touched their lips, they never looked into my eyes or acknowledged my presence. Sometimes a spoon or bowl would slip from my hands to the wooden floor and they would jerk and cry out, startled. They never showed the slightest response to my words though; their eyes remained empty and their faces flaccid.

But Laurent, I knew, understood my words. He would sometimes, after I stated an opinion as to how he wasn't "really trying" or made a casual comment such as "wasn't it nice to see the sun today," bestow upon me a glance of disdain, frustration, even mocking humor, but never did I see in those golden-brown eyes a hint of hope. And never a grunt, a groan, or a harrumph, much less a word, did I ever hear from him. But he and I did communicate and often shared afternoon tea together. He sometimes listened with patient eyes as I would describe the state of the brothers or what I had just found on the front steps from Henri. I imagined that I was company for him and that he realized how very important it was that he recover and go home to a life I felt must be full of promise. There were people waiting for his return, and I would help him return to them. I was a nurse and he the embodiment of all I could hope to heal. His life would be salvaged from the waste and destruction. There would be hope.

In late October, I caught sight of Henri from an upstairs window just as he stepped upon the wagon to depart. I flew down the stairs and out the door to catch him and ask if he could possibly bring me three or four chairs next time. I wanted to set them on the landing at the top of the stairs where the boys might sit by the stove for meals followed by exercise. All three were at last making gains. Laurent was now able to walk alone. Slowly and with care, he walked himself round and round the landing twice a day while I worked with the brothers. They were gaining weight and growing stronger. With great physical support I was able to walk the other two about their rooms and knew I could take them to the landing and onto a chair. There, together, might they show some sign of past acquaintance? Would some slight recollection be stirred if they were in close proximity one to another? Or just by one another's presence might they not be inspired to try harder? Henri said he would bring me chairs in two weeks.

Laurent could also now independently use his chamber pot. I would find evidence each day that his food was passing. The other boys, while often still soiling themselves, were beginning to acquiesce to the routine of finding the pot placed beneath them four times each day—an hour after each meal and the last ritual at the day's end—one then the other. The surveillance of their hygiene, keeping them clean and dry, was my most challenging task. Although the brothers seemed not to have any awareness that they were soiling themselves, I felt a loss of dignity for them that did not lessen with time. Searching their eyes and faces, I hoped to see a sense of shame or apology, an acknowledgment that might move them toward self-awareness that might hasten their movement toward skills needed to go home and be themselves.

But as pleased as I was that Laurent was using the chamber pot by himself and the others most of the time with assistance, there was little to encourage me that any of them either cared, or would eventually care, about what happened to them. I realized much of what I stubbornly regarded as signs of healing were in reality due to abiding by my strict routines. Still, I held fast to any slight indication that they were benefitting from my tending.

Henri brought my four chairs in two weeks' time as promised. Four unmatched seats in many stains of brown, sturdy, high-backed chairs with no side arms. We carried them up the stairs and placed them against the wall in the long L of the landing opposite the stove, two on the north wall and two on the west under the landing's window. I moved the table from Laurent's room and placed it between those chairs. For morning breakfast, the boys sat under the window, the table pulled close between them. If I placed the bowl in front of Laurent and handed him his spoon, he would feed himself while I fed the brothers. After meals, Laurent would walk the landing, passing beside me back and forth as I walked one boy and then the other. I took to singing songs and reciting poems and rhymes. Hearing the sound of my own voice was tiresome, and I would have thought they would be tired of it as well, for no voice other than my own ever filled that landing.

At the beginning of November, after all those weeks of round-the-clock tending, habits were being formed as a result of my efficient daily schedules and routines. I truly felt progress was being made! They had gained weight eating the variety of foods I placed in front of them, seldom soiled themselves, and were able to walk with support. Laurent was even more independent. I now set a goal for them and for myself. They would be well enough to return to their homes by Christmas. This, I realized, was as much out of my own selfish need to return to my solitary life as it was from a compassionate heart. I was becoming weary of being the only one holding out hope. My care was often frayed with impatience.

As the end of November approached, we took all our meals together on the landing, followed by as vigorous exercise as I could extract from each of them. But if only they would give me some sign that they knew they were getting better! Show some spark of cognition, some desire to move out of their present states of apathy. But I continued to assume some sense of hope for us all.

My conviction that they all were headed home was rooted in Laurent's growing independence. Lately, he ended his round of walking about the landing by standing at the top of the stairs looking down. Was he wanting to go explore the house? Maybe a walk outside? Although I encouraged him to venture downstairs with me, he physically resisted and would become tense at my hand on his elbow in invitation to descend the stairs. Shrugging off my hand, he always turned away back toward his room. Of course he was hesitant and most likely even afraid. For what would he find once he left this familiar upstairs abode? I could not know if he realized, as I did, that he would very soon be ready to move on.

I was doing my utmost to give them all I could, all I had. And while their physical needs were being met, I had little to give in the way of any emotional support. So on and on my words of encouragement beat against their ears. Why were they not trying harder? Did they not know I was sacrificing myself for them? I was doing them all the justice I could!

Each morning, I felt myself reset. Today, I vowed, I would be more patient, not so demanding. Each morning as we began our breakfast routine on the landing, I recited to them the day of the week, the month, and the year; what season it was; and a description of the weather outside. I explained the plan for the day, although "the plan" never varied to any great degree, other than perhaps what we would eat for dinner or that it was a Monday and that meant a shave. I hoped the habitual grounding to present might begin to nudge them toward a future.

Had their ability to be present fled along with their spirit, leaving these bodies suspended here in a time and space they were not meant to be? If I dwelled on this, often what seemed the greatest reality during this time, I would wonder if I was not their antagonist, prolonging their stay in this present hell. But on and on we went, for whatever else were we to do?

As December loomed close and days were short on light and long on length, I began to take the boys afternoon tea once again in their rooms. I sat and talked with each of them separately for just a time. The days were cold, and though their doors were left open and the stove's swirling heat flowed to each of their rooms, I knew they were warmest tucked in bed until our communal dinnertime and exercise on the landing.

Laurent always had his tea last, as I wanted to believe he looked forward to this time and found it socially pleasant rather than just a routine to be adhered to. I had begun to share with him stories of my life before the war. I still believed I saw a glimmer of cognizance, of some emotion, when I talked with him about my family in Marseille.

He would now on occasion look at me directly, sometimes for long periods of time, especially if my own eyes were averted from his as I poured our tea or straightened his bedding. I know I asked too often for him to try and talk, to please attempt to tell me the name of his family. Could he but write it on the paper I provided? But he would stare at me and would neither nod nor shake his head at questions I asked.

By the end of the day, my own self tired and worn out, I felt Laurent was being stubborn and was purposefully annoying me. There seemed understanding beyond his eyes, but how was I to know? So on that day, as other days, I took the afternoon tea tray to his room. When I walked in announcing today was chamomile accompanied by bread and jam, he was not in his bed. He was not in the room at all. I placed the tea tray on the dresser and moved back to look on the landing, calling his name. Although he still would sometimes stand atop the landing, I had never seen him attempt any movement to go down the stairs. Having just come from the kitchen, I knew he was not on the lower floor.

As I reentered his room, I noticed that the faded yellow curtains I had found in the bottom dresser drawer and had so recently hung with small nails above the window's frame were rising and fluttering in the cold breeze flowing from the open window.

How had I not seen that open window when I first walked in nor felt the freezing air?

How had I missed the rope tied round the foot of that heavy bed? The rope extending out the open window with what I knew to be Laurent at the other end.

I had not missed those signs when I first entered. Rather, my mind refused to acknowledge the unthinkable vision it conjured.

Standing as frozen in my place as the air in the room, I could not look away from the flapping yellow curtains or the rope stretched and taut against the window ledge. No movement could I make to that window. I did not need to confirm by sight what I knew lay against the house. I turned and closed the door, hoping against hope that Henri, now two weeks since a visit, would come quickly.

The other men did not receive their afternoon tea that day, or the next. I was barely able to feed them their meals and keep them clean. All the daylight hours not spent in tending were spent pacing in and out of the house looking north and then south. Henri needed to come and come now.

Laurent was left dangling high in the frozen air for two full days when, finally, Henri came late the afternoon on the third day. While still a far ways off to the north, I waved with frantic arms and called his name to hurry, hurry. As he came closer, I ran to the wagon and told him what he would find behind the house.

Leading Donkey and his wagon across the side yard round to the back and cutting through the dead lavender stalks, he maneuvered the wagon close against the wall. Standing atop the wagon, he cut the taut rope and set Laurent free. Finally. Henri gently laid him out across the wagon's top and covered his body with a cloth pulled from the back and, with a length of rope, tied it all down.

I was dry of eye. Beyond grief. Henri spent some time assuring me all would be taken care of. He wanted me to know there was no fault here, only the result of a decision made by Laurent alone. Henri said he would return in three days. I made him promise. Promise that it would be three days and no more.

"Yes, yes! Three days, for then it will be December." I did not understand his meaning but only that he would soon return.

This is not how I wanted these boys to leave. This was not justice! Laurent did not do justice to my nursing. Self-righteous indignation filled me with anger and masked the grief and despair I desperately needed contained.

I began over the next days to understand that Laurent had been biding his time. Waiting until he was physically able to climb down those stairs to secure the hanging rope. He would have seen me out his west window as late as the end of September into October hanging our laundry from that rope. Then, in late October, too cold for hanging clothes outside, he could have seen me taking it down and coiling it round and round itself, laying it on the stone slab next to the pump. In all the times since, when filling or emptying pots, pitchers, or buckets, moving indoors and out, I had not missed that rope. He must have hidden it under his bed.

After two days, I ventured into Laurent's room. I untied the rope wound round the bed's leg and burned it outside with the yellow curtains. Then I cleaned that vacant room. Scrubbed on hands and knees every surface, every corner till my knuckles bled and my bare knees were raw and splintered. The wood was wet and the mattress lay propped against the open window for airing. The bedding was washed and now lay hung all across the banister, drying by the stove on the landing.

On the morning of the third day, I made the bed with fresh linens, and I vowed that I would sleep there every night. It would become my room now. Even as I prepared it, I was puzzled by my decision to take the room for myself. I only knew I must, and doing so was somehow a gesture of acknowledgement on both our parts. I trusted Laurent would have wanted me to have this room for my own. A room where we once took our tea together. A room that would not be left vacant even with his passing.

Henri returned as promised on the afternoon of that same day.

"The Sisters arranged all for our friend Laurent. As they prepared his body, they much remarked on his improved state. For even in his demise there was evidence of your good tending, Mademoiselle Marie."

I told Henri I was now going to claim that bedroom as my own. Henri only nodded. Even though I knew I might find solace in his kind eyes, I could not meet his gaze and risk losing my composure. Henri was leaving again, and there would be no one to grieve with other than myself.

He asked after the other two boys. Henri and I had not truly talked since they had arrived in September, but we now exchanged more words than at any time since. I shared with him that their physical state seemed well repaired but there was still no sign of true life, no movement of the face or eyes to validate any presence of spirit. He said he would share all this with the Sisters, as they were renewing efforts to reunite soldiers with their families. We talked specifically of their height, unique coloring of hair, and almost golden eyes, and how they so closely resembled one another. All this he would pass on to the Sisters in the hope of helping find their loved ones.

He slowly unloaded more wood by my back door, wanting, I think, for us to find that place returned to some normalcy. After unloading additional provisions, he climbed aboard his wagon with a quiet adieu. I gave Donkey a quick, fierce hug as he began to pull the weight of the wagon forward.

I sorely wanted to run after Henri and ask when I could expect him next, but I did not want to burden him or acknowledge to myself my need. So I stood my place. I knew he would not be long away but long enough for me to perhaps gain an equilibrium.

Turning my efforts to the remaining boys, I exercised them now three or four times a day, sang louder, and spoke with more feeling. I no longer felt resentment or forced obligation for their care but rather an emerging sense of empathy. Laurent's death had somehow moved me past a point in my own suffering. I could grasp hold of theirs and acknowledge them as separate, sentient beings who somehow could be touched by compassion rather than betrayed by resentment and guilt. Laurent had taught me that I wanted to live. I did not fully know that until his demise, and this was his gift to me for the care I had given.

By March, the brothers were getting out of bed independently, walking the landing, and pausing at the window to view spring's arrival. They were eating all their meals without aid, dressing with minimal help, and using the chamber pot when reminded. Still, they had no voice, but they had one another and seemed content and even peaceful in each other's company. They no longer cried out in their sleep.

In early April, Henri told me the Sisters thought they had made contact with their family. Based on the descriptions I had provided, everyone felt they had found a match. They were indeed brothers. Twins, in fact.

Two weeks later, the brothers rode away, sitting beside Henri atop his wagon. Their faces were still passive, but physically they looked well fed and healthy. Their families were traveling to the convent where they would be reunited. I declined the Sisters' kind invitation to come as well to meet the family and, as I knew, to accept the gratitude they were sure to offer. I had no need to extend the goodbyes, but still I stood in the road and waved them on their way until I could no longer see the wagon.

Upon their departure, I was left with redemption. Redemption for both Laurent and myself. He healed to where he alone could make a choice whether to live or end his life. I tended him without realizing he moved toward a destiny he felt was his. Tended him until he was physically able to decide his own fate and strong enough to carry out his decision. And this was justice after all.

For the first time since his death, I wept for Laurent and then for all our lost men and women and their waiting families forever changed. I wept knowing I had made a choice to live. I silently thanked those boys for allowing me to find my own renewal as I took care of them. And I thanked Henri, who seemed to know all things.

With the warmer days of spring, my spirit continued to thaw. It was a slow thaw, but I felt it starting at the edges. And then, in early June, I received a letter from Solange telling me she was coming to visit my "lavender house in Meuse."

CHAPTER 11

WHEN SOLANGE CAME TO VISIT, JULY 1921

The days before Solange's visit slipped past in silence and were indistinguishable one from the other. Whereas once the sound of my voice was heard continually, speaking words of encouragement and loudly singing songs to the boys, now there was stillness. I felt as empty as the house. I kept thinking I needed to get everything ready for my sister's visit, but in truth there was really nothing to prepare. I had again swept and scrubbed the house, and the beds in the second bedroom, where she would sleep, were made up with clean linens. Other than the bedroom furniture upstairs, the house was still essentially bare of furnishings of any kind. At least the upstairs reflected some semblance of life being lived. Even if it was just to sleep!

Since the boys had gone, the kitchen lay virtually empty and unused. I had little food stored and nothing prepared for my sister's arrival. Henri had been by a week before, but I had not purchased much in the way of supplies or foodstuffs then. I did tell him Solange was coming, and I would need to buy from him the following week. I had not seen him since. Solange and I would decide what we would eat when she got here. However, unless Henri came soon, the reality was that there was virtually nothing to feed my guest! I did not spend much effort in rousing myself to usefulness and, other than the thorough cleaning, had spent each day since receiving her letter listlessly awaiting her arrival.

The joy that accompanied the reunion of the boys with their family and my hope that the worst of my despair had left with them was short-lived. The long days of light and warmth surely should have spurred me to . . . to what? Plant a garden (Henri offered seeds), sew curtains for the newly cleaned and empty rooms upstairs, take a book and my lunch and sit by the river?

The familiar malaise had gradually descended over me. I did not know what to do with myself now that the house was empty again. Even knowing Solange most likely expected to see me well and productive hadn't prompted me to any action. "Productive" was a word she used a great deal when describing the attributes of one living a life in a "healthy manner." She knew I was expecting her, knew that I once again had a house void of life. I had written to her and Papa more frequently during the months the boys shared my house, and she knew all three were gone.

Maybe I was just lazy and not truly fatigued. I had since bumped the mattress from my room on the second floor back down to the first. The distance up and down the stairs mornings and night required more from my person than I had to give, and it was much more difficult sleeping where Laurent had slept than I had imagined. Truth be told, it was difficult to sleep up or down. I just couldn't seem to settle my mind enough to drift off. Maybe it was too quiet. The last nine months of purposefulness and the company of others, even of those who were essentially silent, were extinguished when the boys left. Whereas once the solitude was healing, now it became oppressive. My old sense of restlessness was gnawing at my edges again. I thought this perhaps a good sign—better to feel restless than useless!

I sat on my steps each evening looking over at the Meuse and waiting for Solange. The sound of the river's flow over rocks and roots accompanied the beating of my heart, and if I listened with eyes closed, I could hear the stalks of my brilliant lavender waving over and over themselves in the gentle breeze moving across the vast fields. Solange's letter of three weeks ago said to expect her today or tomorrow, or maybe the next day. I found I was both dreading and eagerly anticipating her arrival. I wanted her to love my home, my land, my river, and to love me as she always had.

The next day arrived hot and bright. Mid-afternoon found me sitting once again on the front steps, hoping for a river breeze, when I heard the sound of metal on wood. I saw the dust rising before the flatbed wagon appeared. Solange was sitting high atop the wagon's seat behind a muscular black-brown beast of a horse. She slapped the reins up and down as though she could see the prize in sight and was driving hard to claim it. Her wide-brimmed, dark navy bonnet was tied with matching sateen sashes blowing wildly about her face.

Solange driving a wagon and heading for my home! I could not help but smile! Ah, my dear sister, almost here to rescue me. I was thankful for the fourteen months of separation, for any sooner visit I could not have welcomed. I stood and waved wildly at her approach, filled with relief and an overwhelming sense that now I could lie down and rest in the presence of her good senses.

She slowed when she caught sight of me, reining in the horse as the dust settled down about her. Her slow approach allowed us to rein in our emotions as well, I think—to focus on one another from afar and perhaps gauge how best to begin our reunion.

She pulled the wagon close alongside me and jumped down, out of breath as though she had run with the horse. "I made good time!" she exclaimed, tying the reins to the hitching post Henri had set close to my steps months earlier. "Actually having never driven a wagon before I think it went rather well."

She folded me into her arms, and I was speechless, not from emotion but from a wave of overwhelming weariness that settled over me. The dust stirred up by the wagon wheels was now clouding all about us, filling our eyes and noses. That is how I felt inside: dusty and dry. And Solange was here to help clean out my cobwebs.

After moving only a few steps back from the wagon, we sat down together as close as possible on the steps, linked our arms, and gazed over at the river. The warmth of her body felt like peace before sleep came, and I laid my head on her narrow shoulder. I even dozed off, apparently, for as the breeze came up, I startled awake. Solange let out a small chuckle and patted my hands, saying it was time to go inside. I knew there was no more delaying her look about my house, and so we rose and walked up the steps to the front door.

She walked ahead of me, moving with determined purpose, and opened the door. She paused just inside, looking left and right, up and down, and began slowly moving through each empty room downstairs. I watched as her eyes took stock of the barren rooms. There were tears at the edge of her words as she began making a verbal list of all we would need to purchase to fill them.

Solange continued talking, making one-sided conversation, not disguising well her concern at finding the house so empty. I did not take on her worry; I was too caught up in the joy at simply hearing her long-missed voice, taking pleasure in every syllable she uttered. It didn't matter that I neither desired nor needed more than what I already had. Seeing the house through her eyes and knowing her opinion of what "every adequate home must have," I realized my house must have appeared barely sufficient to sustain life. She hadn't yet realized there was no life to sustain? Or maybe the house told her its secrets and they were so hard for her to hear. But I let her go on and on.

"Papa was so wise to have purchased the wagon and horse and have it waiting when I arrived. He said it was about time you had your own means of transportation rather than having to rely on the peddler."

So the wagon with horse was Papa's idea. Of course it was! I had no idea what I would do with my "transportation" but I was pleased that the idea had been Papa's. Another gift he thought I needed that he could provide. I had been very disappointed when Solange wrote that he would not be accompanying her on this visit.

She spoke of so many things we needed to accomplish that I finally asked her how long she was planning to stay and where was Papa.

"You know I left Papa in Portugal. We only just completed all the finalities regarding leasing the house in Marseille. We'll be sailing for New York in one month's time." She looked into my eyes and took my hands in hers. "We have no return plans, Marie. I could not leave without seeing you, especially since it may be a long while before we return. I hope it is all right if I stay two weeks."

"Two weeks! Is that all after so much time apart? It will take you at least that long to tell me everything you and Papa have been up to and all your plans! Just two weeks before you leave and go to America?" I said all this with a lightness

I did not feel. Hugging her again and looking into her eyes, I said, "You know I may not let you go, Solange. It is very hard to imagine that you will no longer be just a train's distance away from me."

"After two weeks I promise you will be sick and tired of my harping and nagging. But, yes, I am sad as well but am so glad we do have this time together. We will make the very most of it!"

She finished her walk about the front rooms and headed toward the kitchen. I dreaded her stepping into its barren closeness. After the brothers' departure, my kitchen became desolate once more in every sense of the word. I had once again closed the window shutters, and it took on its former gloom. My kitchen never saw the light, never changed, was always predictable—never caused a shift of light away from a predictable center.

And here Solange went, tsk-tsking and throwing the window shutters and then the back door open wide. She stood and surveyed the pump, the lean-to, and the shed where my nine hens were all stirred up by our racket, clucking louder than Solange was tsk-tsking. How I had missed that sound! All my life, there was no end to all of the reasons my sister had to "tsk" at me. A sound of love.

She walked off the back stoop and past the lean-to to where the fields began and, with her hands on her hips, let out an "ahhh" as she surveyed the fields upon fields of purple lavender. She reached for my hand, and we stood together looking as far as our eyes could see. I was so glad she too appreciated the loveliness of the flowers. After many minutes, she turned us round and we reentered the kitchen, light now illuminating the wooden emptiness of that sparse room with its splintered old table and bench and spider-filled webs along all the empty shelves. Seeing it through her eyes, it really was depressing and completely drab without any color whatsoever. But I was protective of this room, this unkitchen, and I wanted it to continue to lie undisturbed, for it was not yet ready to receive what it could not sustain.

"After we thoroughly clean and stock these shelves, your kitchen will be better in no time," she said as though she had come to nurse my home back to health.

Before we went upstairs, I prompted her to bring in her belongings from the wagon. Later, I told her, we would move the wagon to the back of the house off the road, settle the horse in the lean-to, and then take a walk along the river. She agreed, and we went out again in the bright sunshine and began unloading a half-filled wagon of surprises for me. First, we brought in her luggage and bags, including a large leather travel valise, which I realized was a very old one Papa had used on his travels for as long as I could remember. I wondered if I opened it and put my nose inside would it smell of Papa? Would he then be here for just a little while?

Solange had also managed to bring a very large wooden box and two large rattan baskets of breads, cheeses, teas, dried meats, and fruit. We laid everything on the floor just inside the door. From Papa's valise, Solange pulled a rectangular checked cloth, which we spread across the kitchen table and upon which she placed her baskets of food. That was a worry I could let go of, for she had brought our supper . . . and breakfast, and most likely enough food for many meals.

Standing in the kitchen looking back into the front room, I surveyed the wooden box, Papa's valise, and her pieces of luggage strewn all about. After being empty for so long, the room now seemed cluttered and almost made me uneasy.

"And now to move the wagon and then to your river," Solange said, and we strolled out the front door to the road, arm in arm. Now that she was here, my dependable take-charge sister, all seemed more right with the world. And now it was my turn to show her my world.

Together we led the horse round to the back of the house, unhitched him from his trappings, gave him a quick brushing, and settled him into the lean-to. Our next task was to transport the two heavy metal buckets of grain and two bales of fresh grass hay from the back of the wagon to the horse. I was sure Papa had also arranged for the hay and grain to ensure his gift-horse would be fed!

Solange climbed into the wagon and handed down the grain, after which I climbed into the wagon with her and together we managed to heave the hay over the side and drag the bales into the shed. I must admit it felt good to be doing work this physically challenging. It was also surreal that I would be in the countryside in Meuse unhitching a horse from a wagon (both now mine!), heaving hay, and lifting buckets with Solange. Without a word spoken, I knew when she looked at me these same incredulous thoughts were going through her head as well. Who would ever have thought our lives would have changed so drastically from the ones we led together in Marseille? With a quick hug for Horse, we brushed the hay from our clothes, bid the hens adieu, and set off for my river.

I was glad the afternoon was bright and shining, the sun's rays dancing over the surface of the water giving a festive welcome to my sister. I had brought my blanket from the house, and at my favorite spot we spread it on the grassy bank. With our backs leaned up against the poplar trees, we listened to the Meuse gurgling over the rocks and to our own and each other's unspoken thoughts.

"Are you happy here, Marie?"

I thought for some time before answering. "I am certainly not unhappy," I said, looking out at the river. "I think I am mostly content. But since the boys have left I must admit I am, while not really lonely, maybe wondering what I will do with myself. I feel somewhat at loose ends."

"Mmm. That makes sense, you know. From your letters Papa and I knew how busy you were. Your dedication to your wards was evident, so it is natural after having been so occupied physically and mentally for you to think about how you might now fill your days. It surely is an adjustment."

"They left in May and here it is July, and I cannot seem to find the energy to even think about what to do next. Mostly I just want to sleep. Is that strange?" I asked.

"No, not strange at all. You most likely need a good rest. And then, of course, there was Laurent." She placed her hand upon mine and leaned toward me. "Hopefully you know it was not your fault that he chose to end his life as he did."

I let out a long sigh and took a moment to examine my feelings. "I have seen so much death and suffering, and despite all the best efforts of myself and others, we could do nothing to save so many of them. I realized shortly after arriving at the front that I was not responsible for whether the soldiers ultimately lived or died. Nurse's training instilled that reality in us all. We had to live that perspective, otherwise we would not have been able to do our jobs. And I did my job as best I could every day. There is no question in my mind that I was a good nurse.

"My struggles now continue to be coming to terms with the extent of the dying, trying to answer questions about the necessity of it, and attempting to make some sense of it all. I am better able now, with the passing of time, to separate my nursing experiences from my personal emotions. But that presents other problems I can't seem to sort out. I keep asking myself if the war really made a difference. What did all those lost lives accomplish? It would be far easier if I could just fit it all together into a single compartment in my mind that said 'professional nurse.' I can't seem to do that, and when I am not busy, as I am not now, my mind asks those questions again and again. I think that is what makes me weary. I am tired of the questions."

"Papa says all thoughtful people are asking those same questions, Marie. Now that life has resumed some perceived sense of normalcy, Papa hears those conversations in the cafés and at the appointments he attends. It is interesting to spend time outside of France listening to people in countries not so affected by the conflict reflect on what has occurred. Sometimes what I hear is offensive, and I feel the fierce loyalty I have always felt for France. Other times I can't help but ask those same questions myself. And Papa does as well. The difference is that you saw it firsthand; your hands were bloodied by the reality of what was lost. And what was gained? That remains to be seen. I tell myself we are free from the tyranny that would have been had we not found victory. That is my only answer to the question of why. Real or not, it is what I hold on to." Solange leaned back once more against the tree and closed her eyes.

Because of my isolation I had supposed it was easy to think that others may not have been in much the same state as myself. Back in Marseille, people had seemed jubilant at the war's end and rightfully so. I just didn't imagine they could also be questioning at the same time. And then coming here there was no one with whom to discuss the state of affairs post-conflict. I had thought I did not even want to talk about any of it but found that this conversation with Solange was indeed welcome. She gave me permission not to feel responsible for being the sole individual trying to make sense of a changed world.

Henri had offered to bring me newspapers, assuming I might want to know about what was happening beyond this house in Meuse. He also probably thought a broader perspective outside of myself might help alleviate my gloom. Maybe I was now more interested and ready than I had thought to resume discourse outside of my depressing, one-sided, internal conversations. Solange had only been here a few hours, but already her presence and our conversation was lifting months of dullness from my brain and body. The sun was settling into the river now, and I was getting hungry. I kept imagining what lay in the baskets of food on my old kitchen table.

"Solange, are you awake?" I knew she wasn't, as I had earlier heard her breathing settle into the familiar sound of her sleeping. More than an hour had passed, she dozing and I lost in my own thoughts and just enjoying her here with me by the river. But my stomach had another agenda.

"Solange, wake up and let's go eat. I know you must be as hungry as I am," I said, shaking her gently.

"Yes, yes," she said with some annoyance at being shaken awake. "Is it always so peaceful here? What a wonderful place for an afternoon slumber. We must do this every day I am here."

I nodded my agreement and held out my hand to help her rise. We shook out the blanket and took off for the house. Again, I felt pride that my sister was already enjoying the tranquil beauty of this place.

"It is certainly a good thing that you brought food, as I had nothing to eat," I said as we entered the house. "I did expect Henri to come before your arrival so I would at least have something." I began rummaging through the overflowing baskets.

"Oh yes. Henri. I want to hear more about this peddler Henri, and so does Papa. Why have you not purchased a cart or wagon before so you could go into town and get what you need rather than rely on a stranger? And obviously you could do with some more household effects," she said, looking around again at the empty rooms.

"Well, Henri stopped early on when I first arrived and has been doing so every week or so for all this time. I have never needed or wanted to go into town and have been perfectly happy getting what I need from him. Really, Solange, he has been most helpful. Especially when the boys were here and I needed supplies and foodstuffs weekly. He also brought me the hens, so I always had fresh eggs to eat and for barter. There was little I required apart from essentials, and more often than not, Henri supplied additionally what he thought I could use. And I can admit to you but never would to him that he has been a reliable source of goodwill and kindness. Of course, I pay him, but he has never taken advantage and never asks me questions." I stated all of this in what I thought was a very matter-of-fact manner. "I have often wondered if Papa had not somehow contacted Henri and paid him a stipend to keep an eye on me. Do you know if this is true?" I asked.

"Ha! I wondered that myself when your letters describing Henri first arrived, but when I asked Papa, he assured me he knew nothing of the man and has even been quite concerned given that Henri seems to be rather over-solicitous on your account. Truth be told, Papa is very much hoping I will have a chance to meet this individual and report back my impressions," she said with a half-smile on her lips.

I found myself laughing at the thought that Henri could ever be perceived as a suspicious character and told Solange so.

"He is well known to the Sisters at the convent not far from here, as well as to all those living north and south on this road. He has been, I think, in the business of traveling commerce, as he calls it, for most of his life. But I ask him as few questions as he asks me, so I do not really know. I told him you were coming for a visit and that we would need supplies, so I really do expect him any day."

As if on cue, Henri and Donkey rambled up the road the next morning as we were finishing our breakfast and making a list of all Solange thought we would need for my house; we were planning a shopping trip into town with my new transportation. Anticipating Henri's momentary arrival, I experienced a twinge of nervousness in my stomach, wondering what he and Solange would make of one another. And wondering also why it seemed to matter. I did know that up until then, Henri made my life here possible, and should Papa receive an unfavorable report from Solange, there might be difficulties. Yes, I definitely needed this meeting of these two important people in my life to go well.

"Bonjour, Henri!" I called out loudly, to ensure he would indeed stop and engage us. He smiled and got down from the cart as I approached Donkey with my usual welcoming hugs, and I introduced them both to Solange.

"Bonjour, mesdemoiselles," Henri said, removing his hat from his head and bowing slightly to my sister. I thought his hair was trimmed shorter and was freshly washed perhaps?

Solange acknowledged his greeting and then we all stood as though not quite knowing what to say next. My stomach churned, realizing that Henri and Solange were appraising one another. My two benefactors face-to-face, with me just standing there.

I had nine eggs ready in my basket for Henri. Solange had helped me gather them that morning. I wanted her to see that I was indeed using some of my own resources to fend for myself.

"*Merci*, Mademoiselle," said Henri as he took my basket and moved round to the back of the wagon. He unlocked the hinges to lay open the back. Henri often brought items unexpected and much welcome, and I just knew that because Solange had come he might have more than the usual flour and cheese. Of course, I was not disappointed.

"In celebration of your visit, Mademoiselle, and your sister having told me you have not been to this part of France before, I have taken it upon myself to bring some items that are distinctive to our region of Meuse." He pulled from the recesses of the wagon a large box lined with a blue cotton cloth, the ends folded over so we could not yet see what lay beneath.

"The good Sisters from the convent nearby send you jars of their honey, with the express request that you take some to your papa for his enjoyment as well," he said, setting five small jars on the wagon's lid. He then added, as though it were a surprise to him, "Oh, I see the Sisters have also included three boxes of their beeswax candles. Twelve beeswax *bougies* in all. Not knowing if you had holders for them, I have brought you six *bougeoirs*. These seats for your candles are mismatched, but may you find them decorative as well as useful." He said this plainly, but I saw the twinge of a smile playing round his mouth. I had told him many times that I did not need candles or candleholders, that it seemed an extravagance as I was seldom up after dark.

"How long might you be visiting, Mademoiselle?" Henri asked, placing the jars of honey and the candles back into the box and passing it into Solange's arms.

"Two weeks, Monsieur," Solange said, peering into the back of the wagon.

"I hope, then, that it will be my pleasure to see you again to bid you a good journey home before you leave." Turning to me, Henri asked, "Mademoiselle Durant, what can I bring that you might need, as I will be by again in three days' time?"

"Solange arrived with a horse and wagon that Papa had arranged from Portugal. Papa's gift to me! We are planning a drive into town as soon as we decide on what we need. Solange is encouraging me to fill my house with items she insists might make me more comfortable," I said with a smile while lacing my arm through my sister's.

"Wonderful! A horse and wagon are certainly a necessity for you if you are to continue living here, Mademoiselle. You will find your way around town in no time, and people will be most happy to make your acquaintance, guiding you as best they can to whatever you might require. Whether the items might be available for purchase is another matter. Much is still in short supply. Your *père* is indeed a wise man to have arranged your transportation and your sister kind to make such a prudent delivery." He smiled at Solange and removed his hat once again, then bowed slightly and said, "Bravo to you both, and if there is any way in which I might be of assistance, I would count it my privilege."

He closed the back of the wagon, handed me another basket with what I assumed were the bougeoirs wrapped in heavy paper, and gave Donkey a kind slap on his middle. Then he jumped atop the wagon with a final, "Adieu. See you in three days!" and was off down the road.

We took our new bounty into the house and stacked it all on the small table we had moved downstairs from my room. Solange could not resist opening a jar of the honey, so she reached for that first. I stuck my hand into the basket that held the bougeoirs and found a round loaf of crusty bread Henri had tucked inside as well. I set it on the table and ran to the kitchen where I grabbed two plates and two knives. As quickly as I cut thick slices of bread Solange slathered them with the sweet, fragrant honey.

"Papa will love this! And to think it is made here in the convent by Sisters who live so close to you," she said with her mouth stuffed full.

With these words, I knew she had given her blessing and acknowledged that a good impression had been made, and all was right with my world. Solicitations from the Sisters via Henri and their gifts of the honey and candles were evidence to Solange that I had acquaintance with others besides "the Peddler." I knew it made her feel more comfortable that I was not truly alone here. I did not tell Solange that I had neither visited the convent nor met the good nuns. I was thinking Henri was a clever fellow and, whether knowingly or unknowingly, had once again come to my aid.

We did not go into town that day. Instead, we chose to take a long nap in the sun by the river after we gorged on our bread and honey and took our time finishing our list for what would be our excursion the next day.

As dusk approached, I prepared a light supper. Solange unwrapped the six bougeoirs from the basket and discovered, as I knew she would, that each was a lovely treasure. I set our cutlery out as she finished fitting the last of the candles into its holder, and as I set down our plates of food, she arranged them across the table and lit each wick. I would be sure that several of the bougeoirs made their way into her luggage. I was basking in more than the candlelight, reflecting on the many gifts bestowed on us that day.

Up early the next morning, Solange imparted to me that she clearly recalled how to harness Horse and hitch him to the wagon and would instruct me on the finer points of driving. Truly the novice leading the novice! Thank heavens Horse was a patient and gentle teacher, for he seemed to be guiding us to what we needed to do and how to do it. We three became fast attached that day as we rode the bumpy way north.

In town, we rummaged and sorted through shop after shop, realizing again and again that there was little from Solange's list that was available within the budget I had allocated for purchases. I insisted on paying for it all, albeit from the monies Papa had given me when I first left Marseille, and would accept nothing in the way of funds from Solange. If I could not pay for it, it was not purchased. In this way, I also made sure the number of pieces of furniture and accoutrements were kept to a minimum, as I truly did not want a house filled with things that meant nothing to me and for which I had no need. I also wanted only objects that had been used, that had lived a life before coming to me. I had no use for anything that was new.

We finally found a moderately sized mahogany table for the dining area, four matching chairs, and an almost-matching glass-fronted china hutch. All were scratched and scarred, obviously well used, and I immediately wanted them to find a new home with me. With a thorough cleaning and a heavy coat of the Sisters' rich beeswax polish, they would soon be restored and ready to be loved once again.

Found in another shop, in the depths of a back room that Solange charmed her way into, where she haggled relentlessly with the owner, we secured a tapestried divan in shades of sage and oatmeal, two stuffed armchairs, two lamps, and two small round tables of cherry wood. These pieces, though not new, looked as such, and Solange was triumphant at this find of what she declared was "very suitable indeed." My empty house, where all these pieces would come to live, would now be a suitably appointed home. Too full for my taste, but I knew their presence would provide Solange with a sense that a life was indeed being lived there. If that eased her departure and provided a good report to Papa, I was content.

She also insisted I needed warmer clothes and bought me a long, heavy coat and thick wool hat she said I would most surely need for winter when driving the wagon to and from town. She assured me they were belated birthday gifts, otherwise I would not have accepted them. I next purchased a slightly used pair of heavy boots, two pairs of thick socks, and a wool scarf. Lastly, we bought more grain, hay, and a dark red heavy wool blanket for Horse. Then, feeling weary and triumphant, we eagerly headed home.

During the remainder of Solange's visit, we enthusiastically cleaned and polished our finds, speaking in English as much as we could; she wanted to practice before arriving in America. All the while, we arranged and rearranged the gleaming furniture until she was pleased with the placement of each piece. She insisted we take our tea in the "parlor," as she called the west side of my downstairs area, as she wanted to remember us sitting there together. The east side of the room, where we placed the dining table and chairs, she called my "*salle à manger*," my dining room. I had to admit the pieces did look perfect under the window. We situated the hutch against the wall that separated this larger open space from the kitchen.

On a last foray into town, we purchased enough food, dry goods, and feed for my animals that we did not need to return. Solange found a set of "gently used" china plates and bowls with matching serving pieces, and many cooking utensils, including a flour sieve and rolling pin, adamant that these were essentials in any proper kitchen. I did like the china. It had a delicate pattern of flowers and nearly matched the teacups Henri had brought when the boys were with me. I gently placed each plate and cup into my hutch and stood back, admiring them through the leaded glass doors.

We spent the rest of our time together in lazy conversation. The days were warm and most afternoons found us once again by the river, enjoying the solitude of this beautiful place that seemed more home to me than ever before. My dear sister's initial "tskings" at the sight of the emptiness of my house turned to "ahhhs" of admiration and praise as we decided upon the final arrangement of the acquisitions now gracing my lovely house. We settled in for the final days cooking, sharing stories, laughing, and crying—consciously making new memories for us both to remember and linger on.

Shortly before Solange departed, Henri called upon us once again. That is the only way I can describe his "passing through," as he was very polite and solicitous and did not much offer his merchandise. After some time in conversation, he bid Solange a charming and genteel adieu. I knew that his timing was intentional and was grateful for his kindness toward my sister.

"Not a bad fellow, this Henri," was all she had to say as we stood together watching Donkey and him travel down the road. I merely smiled, nodding my agreement.

I drove the wagon myself that last day to see Solange boarded on the early-afternoon train headed west and back to Papa. Our visit had been more than I could have hoped. Our goodbyes were tearful, each of us reassuring the other that we would, of course, write as always and with the promise that we would see each other in the not so distant future. As I pulled away from the station and back toward home, I felt a sense of melancholy and some astonishment that she and Papa were truly leaving for America within the next few weeks. So far away from what they had always known. But had I not done the same? Moved body and soul to this place far away from all that was familiar? And I had told Solange the truth: I was truly content.

Beyond that, knowing Solange had come and gone and bestowed her blessing here, I allowed myself to fully embrace this place I had chosen as home. I did not know how my days would be filled, but I did know I had a companiable horse, nine laying hens, a good-sized wagon, a well-supplied kitchen, and a home full of furniture to care for. That was more than enough for now.

CHAPTER 12

THE SEWING BOX, OCTOBER 1921

One of Solange's gifts for me had been our large sewing box from home, which she said she had restocked with new needles, many spools of thread, freshly sharpened shears, my worn and perfectly fitted thimbles, and "bits and pieces" she thought I would find use for.

I had neither touched nor moved, much less opened, the box during or since her visit. Lifting it now, three months on, I remembered it was very heavy, but it seemed even heavier than I recalled from home. Indeed, the sewing box had beckoned me since Solange's departure—a distraction that drew my eyes each time I passed it, set so innocently atop my dining table. I began imagining its contents, perhaps filled with alluring items of color and texture. But I was busy, much too busy to go through it and idle my time away with needlework! I had become quite good at making excuses for not delving into and exploring the inside of this sewing box.

Needlework was always a pastime we enjoyed. Solange called it "relaxing creativity," and it was certainly a fine way to pass many a winter's day into evening by our hearth. She chided me often over my basket, overflowing with half-finished projects of embroidery and crewel. The planning of projects and the initial coming together of them was where I found the pleasure. The feel of the vibrantly colored textures and varying hues of thread across my hands as it slipped in and out of my fingers and was woven through fabrics of silk, satin, linen, and wool engrossed my senses. I could become lost in creating the beginning form of a tapestry, my stitches tight, even, and perfectly formed.

Once the colors and form began to take shape and I could see the final piece clearly in my mind's eye, the repetitiveness toward completion became boring and tedious. Solange, however, finished every project she began. She planned it thoroughly before even threading a needle and enjoyed the process and detail of the work; each piece evolved into a unique, completed expression of herself. She might work on two or three pieces simultaneously but, unlike myself, no project was ever left to wait for an inspired hand to see it to its beautiful end.

Over a single change of seasons, pillow and chair covers, table runners, and tablecloths of various sizes were finished and placed in the large wooden box and then delivered as donations to the charity holiday bazaar in late fall. Our needlework was highly esteemed, and we had eager patrons vying to purchase and asking for "just an early peek" at what we would be offering for sale each winter.

I often imagined that these loyal customers from year to year presented our handiwork as gifts to relatives who never knew that the delicate and intricate artistry came from any hands other than those of their own dear *tantes* or *grand-mères*. My caustic comments on the subject always brought a smile to Solange's lips, but she never remarked other than to make me promise to complete a project of my choice at least every two months throughout the year. By choosing smaller items—short table runners and small pillow coverings— thereby reducing the tedium, I was able to discipline myself and contributed considerably to our cache of finished products ready for donation and sale. Those I could accomplish quickly and still make my quota.

As I worked on these small pieces, I began experimenting with unique variations of color and texture. After some time I became frustrated, unable to create with the fabric and thread what I had envisioned in my mind. Solange would say that she believed I had an "artistic bent," and the following spring she employed an old man to teach me drawing and watercolors. He smelled of mothballs and always had bits of pipe tobacco stuck in his salt-and-pepper mustache, which completely covered his upper lip. He mumbled when he spoke and, able only to see a bottom lip, I often had no clue as to what he was saying. It soon became clear that his mumbles consisted primarily of comments about my "unconventional use of form and color." He seemed at a loss as to what to do with his atypical student. After Solange told him that he must persevere and, I am sure, increased his payment, he reluctantly introduced me to the medium of oil paints. Here I found what fulfilled my desire to create texture upon texture of vivid color, and form "went out the window with the devil," as my teacher so succinctly informed Solange.

The scent of the paint and turpentine thrilled me as well, but Papa insisted that I was filling the house with "odiferous smells." Solange relegated me to what had been a storage room on the second floor where I could create among the pungent fumes to my heart's content. This became my "studio," and I loved the hours spent lost in this other world. No one referred to my pieces as art, but this creative outlet filled me with an excitement and a sense of accomplishment that I had not previously experienced. I would later realize that Solange would support any endeavor that eased my restless spirit and kept me home.

I had spied a long wooden table at the wharf, of a perfect height for standing and painting, and talked a fisherman into selling it to me as well as carting it back to the house. After scrubbing it clean of fish scales and guts, I proceeded to lay across its top in a whirling array all my art supplies. The colors of my oils were vibrant, and I preferred many-hued blues, ochre, yellows, scarlet, and greens. The tabletop was soon smeared with these colors, making a canvas of itself. For the paintings, I used white canvas stretched across small wooden frames, my "*petits tableaux*" Papa called them. Layer upon layer of color created texture into which I often placed bright bits of thread or fabric. My studio began taking on a colorful life of its own as I filled it with my works, which leaned against the walls all about the room.

Solange and I took to having our afternoon tea in my studio, as I would have otherwise skipped it altogether. She dragged in two overstuffed chairs and a colorful little mosaic-tiled table we used out in the garden sometimes and arranged them in front of the adjoining windows. The afternoon light streamed in, playing off the colors of the canvases round the floor and filling the room with a swirling luminescence. After tea, we would work together on our needlepoint—or she might. I often chose to paint instead. When Solange's fingers tired, she would sometimes walk the periphery of the room and pick up a painting, holding it close and then as far out as her arms would stretch. She might comment on the colors or share whatever thoughts crossed her mind as she gazed at the piece. She sometimes stayed until time to begin the preparations for dinner; Papa seemed to invite guests more frequently than ever round this time. I would emerge later as the daylight began to fade, to ready myself for dinner as well. Each morning would find me once again in my studio.

Over time, my small pieces found homes in nooks throughout our house. Solange would choose a piece to display and take it to a woodworker to form a frame of her own design to complement the canvas. The frames always provided a subdued border for the flamboyant middle. The larger pieces she would hang on a space of wall; the small ones she set on a table or leaned up against a well-placed stack of books. I sometimes wondered if our traditionally styled and furnished home of neutral colors and dark woods was at odds with these unexpected bursts of vibrant color.

Eventually, we came to feel my paintings and her frames added interest and a certain modern touch to the otherwise staid interior. Solange, always subtle and very correct, took care to tuck each splash of color into spaces few people other than the three of us would likely encounter. When a visitor did happen on such a surprise, the reactions were varied and curious. Solange and I would smile as Papa explained to the visitor that the *petits tableaux* were my and Solange's creations and were they not truly unique and inspired? We came to love them more because we knew Papa did as well.

And now, here in Meuse, sat this large, displaced, unopened sewing box Solange had left me. I felt she meant to tempt me toward picking up a sharp needle in anticipation of sliding a silky thread through its eye, or perhaps I'd be persuaded by tubes of paint to feast my eyes on colors so bright I might not bear it.

Truth be told, my practical self had reminded me of late that I could really do with an apron or two. I often found myself beginning to wipe my hands down the front of my dress, lost in thought, only to realize I was not wearing an apron. I also felt at a loss when I would walk along my river or among my lavender and go to place a unique pebble or stalk of flower in pockets that were not there. And certainly I needed those pockets to gather my eggs and keep my clothespins. Yes, I missed my aprons and my pockets.

So I did what I always did now when I was in need. I made a request of Henri to secure several meters of a plain muslin cloth from which I could make a few aprons. I could have taken myself to town and scoured the shops for the material, but it was simpler to explain to Henri, and as always, he exceeded my request, both to my amazement and to my consternation.

Within two weeks he presented me with about fifteen-to-twenty meters of raw material: a bolt of traditional beige muslin with tan and brown flecks, tightly woven and of a thickness that would easily take a needle and still hold its shape. I suggested we cut off only what I needed for three aprons, approximately five meters, and then he could sell the remainder of the bolt. Surely there was a great demand for the fabric, as it had been scarce during and now after the war.

"Yes, a good plan, Mademoiselle Marie, but I have a better one through which we both will profit! Since you asked me about the cloth to make aprons, I have mentioned here and there to the *mesdames* on my route that I may, within a reasonable period of time, have aprons for them to purchase. They are now waiting with great anticipation to replace their old worn out garments with new. I supply the cloth and you make the aprons. I will sell them and we share the profit! Voilà! A better plan!"

Henri must by now, I realized, be able to predict my reactions: he unequivocally discounted the first words from my mouth after he presented one of his grand schemes. Not one to disappoint, I looked at him directly and delivered a firm if somewhat louder than intended, "No, absolutely not!"

He just stood and patiently waited for me to list, with all the logic I always tried to muster, the numerous reasons that this was not an idea I needed to pursue or was even interested in. I was already trading eggs to barter and was able to purchase other items and food I needed. I was busy enough. Where would the supply of cloth and sewing items continue to come from? I didn't want to spend all my time sewing. How did we know that with all that effort anyone would want to purchase the aprons? And finally, I had never made a complete apron by myself before.

"Yes, yes, all good reasons, I am sure," he said as he transferred the wide bolt of cloth from his arms to mine. It was heavier than I expected.

"Let us begin with five aprons, then. Nothing too ambitious. The war is over, and we must discard those things that harbor remnants of sadness and replace them with that which is new and full of hope. New aprons are just what a new day calls for! Oh, and be sure to cut a few to fit the wider girths of some of our more fortunately endowed *mesdames*."

He tipped his hat to me and climbed aboard the wagon, and Donkey began moving forward slowly before Henri even released the reins from their hook. With what I hoped was a look of great agitation, I abruptly turned and stomped toward my front door. I tried to ignore the feelings of anticipation as my eager fingertips ran lightly across the slightly grainy surface of the muslin in my arms. First, before the thought of any others, I would make one apron and it would be mine.

The next morning, I awoke early to rain pounding loudly on the roof. The wind lashed the water hard against the windows, and I recognized the quick hits of hail as well. A good day for staying indoors. And without much to do, I felt snuggling down into my featherbed a better option than setting feet to cold wood floors. My second thought, that it would be a good day to finally explore my sewing box, I attempted to push aside in lieu of more sleep. But I knew the renewal of hail on the window would make sleeping impossible. Still resisting, I dozed a little longer but woke suddenly, remembering I needed to take care of Horse and the hens, bring in wood, and stoke fires throughout the house. And besides, I was hungry. Eggs and tea might fortify me for my long-procrastinated reacquaintance with that box.

The sense of fear I felt was certainly unreasonable yet very real. What could a sewing box possibly harbor that caused me such trepidation? Chores were completed but hours passed, and I still had not ventured toward it. Finally, past noon, I sat down on the floor with the box in front of my crossed legs. I sighed deeply, then pushed the hook latch to the side, and the lid literally sprang open. How had Solange managed to fill it so full and still set the latch?

Lifting the lid fully open, my senses were immediately assaulted with memories—not from the sight of what was in the box but the smell. Smells evoking memories of home and family. And this was the reason for my fear. Always acute to smells and the associations they called forth, I was overwhelmed with a longing for a time before. Before war and grief and loss rained down upon us all.

Every home I have ever entered was infused with the unique fragrance of that family and its domestic life. When I thought of friends left in Marseille, I could picture them clearly and recall the smell of each house with its particular essence that might be made up of garlic and olive oil, fish or roast, scented candles burning in the foyer, tobacco, or the perfumes worn by those in residence. Occasionally, the family's dog would add to the bouquet.

My sewing box emitted the complex and familiar odors of wood polish, cloves and cinnamon, Papa's pipe tobacco smelling of sweet cherry, and Solange's delicate perfume. No longer hesitant, I excitedly lifted each item gently from its cramped quarters, unwinding or unfolding every treasure, lifting it to smell, feeling the texture between my fingers, and then laying each ribbon, twist of embroidery floss, skein of yarn, and spool of thread round me as I sat there on the floor. Soon I was encircled by reminders of my sister's love and generosity, her knowledge of what I would find fine and beautiful that would entice me toward awareness.

The early afternoon sun broke through the clouds, setting the circle of color ablaze so vividly I had to look away. I hoped my thankful heart transcended the distance to my family. The remaining hours of light I spent slowly exploring the rest of the contents. The box was deep, deeper than I recalled, but then Solange would have removed any items she felt I would not need or want, replacing them with others whole and new.

There in the very bottom was a long, rectangular wooden box with a wrapped bundle tucked close beside it. I knew immediately it contained new oil paints. There were seven tubes in all my favorite colors, all the bright hues I so loved! The wrapped bundle held a variety of brushes, a small palette, my paint knife, and a carving tool. Charcoal sticks and several lengths of colored pastel chalks were included as well. Oh sister, my dear sister. I knew the treasures she chose to place there were tokens of acknowledgement. This box held her kindness, understanding, and permission for me to carry on. I again felt our closeness, our sense of deep caring and love for one another, and was once more thankful for her visit in July. Tomorrow, I would write to her expressing my appreciation. I felt remiss now that I had not opened the box sooner so I could have written her of my gratitude. It would be a welcomed letter, I was sure.

I had bread dough rising in the kitchen and went now to place it in the oven, then out through the back door to gather more wood, which I stacked against the wall just inside the kitchen door. In the evening's last light, needing to remove myself for a brief moment from the memories inside, I ventured out again to stroll around my home. I had had nothing to fear from my sewing box and its memories. Thankfulness and a deep sense of peace, which had with time become my abiding emotions here in my house in Meuse, were only deepened by the knowledge that my memories also included those of another home in what seemed another time, and those memories were welcome here as well.

After walking back to the chicken coop and finding two warm eggs for my dinner (again wishing for a pocket or two) and picking up two more pieces of wood for the stove, I paused at my back door before lifting the latch. Greeting me upon entering was the smell of baking bread, warm fires, and lavender mingling with the lingering scents from my sewing box. This was the fragrance of my home in Meuse.

CHAPTER 13

APRONS, FALL 1921 – WINTER 1921

O nce a year, Solange had us peruse all of our clothes and decide what to keep, what to mend, and, acquiescing to the shifts of fashion for the coming seasons, what to update with a cut and stitch here or lace added there. Depending on our clothing allowance and Papa's plans for future dinner soirées (our appearance had to reflect well on Papa's financial status), we sojourned every three or four months to our favorite dressmaker's shop. Not an event I ever looked forward to. I knew that Solange didn't especially enjoy spending hours looking at fabrics and discussing cuts and lengths, costs and so forth either, but she did it with greater aplomb than I could ever muster. Sighs and groans were my occasional contributions to the swirling conversation surrounding the putting on and pulling off of muslin samples. Only the texture and colors of the fabric were of interest to me, and I chose those carefully, often causing Solange to roll her eyes at my choices, more bold and intricate than the current fashion would dictate. We would compromise when I was in a collaborative mood or the color choices were uninteresting, always leaving Solange to decide the final cut and style of our garments.

We also had a variety of protective smocks for different garments and occasions, ranging from elaborate ones over formal dresses, made by the dressmaker of complementary or matching fabric, to our clean, well-worn, comfortable smocks we wore over housedresses when alone at home.

Our aprons were not above Solange's yearly inspection. We both had our worn favorites and, with the handling of each one, we would tell a snippet of story or remembrance. Remember when Monsieur Robart flung the leg of lamb at his wife just as dinner began, and I mopped his wife's brow clean of the splatter with this apron? See the stains from the wine sauce still here? Oh yes, that apron was to be kept! Or the time Elise decided she would brew mead and it all exploded as it sat aging just behind the furnace. We had been sitting at the kitchen table peeling potatoes when the popping began, sending beer flying out from the furnace and covering everything, including us, with its warm, sticky, dark liquid. We pulled our aprons over our heads and ran for cover! Giving up our aprons tied to such memorable stories or events was so difficult, in fact, that we decided rather than be rid of them we would put them into a chest upstairs along with other favored memorabilia.

Aimée was the seamstress who had made our simple aprons and housedresses when we were younger. She was now an elderly woman and had become a close friend. At least three times a year Solange and I would choose and buy fabrics for Aimée to use, and she would come to the house for tea and lunch. We would spend most of a day or two chatting and cutting patterns together. We had our favorite apron patterns, and occasionally we would change the number of pockets or size and modify the length or cut of the apron. Often I would add a bright spot of color chosen from my many scraps of fabric. Over the many years, Aimée's fingers stiffened and her eyesight faded. I began to do most of the cutting and Solange the finishing stitches. Aimée's only source of income was her sewing, and she would remain our seamstress, if in name only, as long as she was able to come visit and bestow upon us her gracious good nature.

And now, here I was in another time and place, in Meuse, completely alone with no Solange or Aimée to offer direction, contemplating the making of aprons. Eyeing the waiting bolt of muslin Henri had procured for me, I took sketch paper from the sewing box and attempted to duplicate from memory the simple, straight design, cut in one piece with added ties at the neck and waist. Narrow ties of muslin for the neck and a wider set of ties at the waist with both attached to the finished edge of the body of the apron.

Lifting the lid of my sewing box again, I found my measuring tape and stretched the length of it from my collarbone to below my knee. One meter of muslin would do well for a single apron. The rhythmic *thump* of unrolling the heavy bolt across the wooden floor between the divan and the dining table seemed loud in the quiet stillness of the morning. I measured the meter and cut straight across the fabric using a line of floorboard as a guide. My sharp sewing shears vibrated against the wood and up through my hand. Every sense seemed heightened; every stroke of the shears filled me with anticipation mingled with fear. How silly of me! I had been making aprons for as long as I could remember. Yes, but not alone, on a bare wooden floor with only the sewing box and vibrating shears for company, knowing that I would now be the seller of aprons rather than the buyer. This caused me to smile, let go of the fear, and finish the straight cut.

I unfolded the cut fabric and smoothed out the center crease as best I could to check the straightness. I began to feel a remembered sense of eagerness and impatience. Always in my painting and sewing projects—maybe all aspects of life—I found not the final result but the process of creating to be the most exhilarating.

Folding the length of the muslin together again, I picked a piece of drawing charcoal from the sewing box and proceeded to dot cutting lines, marking a narrowing at the curve of underarm and bodice down to a tapered waist and widening again from hips to knees. Making fast work of cutting, shears moving swiftly through the muslin, I soon had my first apron cut. I then cut another, using the first as a pattern.

The flat iron was heating on the stovetop, and a bowl of water lay on the kitchen block ready to sprinkle for steam. First, I ironed the fold into flatness, the scent of water on cloth as it met the hot iron sending a wave of memory as the steam swirled all around me. What a heavenly fragrance! Turning all the edges under wasn't as easy as I had hoped. And although I loved the aroma and feel of hot cloth, the task took much longer than I found interesting.

Thankfully the muslin was a medium thickness, and as long as the iron was hot and the fabric damp, I was able to fold all edges into a hemline. Pinning as I went, it must have taken me well over an hour and several scorched fingers to hem half the apron. I bemoaned again my dark kitchen, deciding that I would do cutting and ironing only on bright days when I could open the back kitchen door for the afternoon's light. But I had forgotten that I could open the shutters of the two kitchen windows. This I did, and fall's rays poured through those panes, infusing my spirit and transforming my kitchen to a place of new light. With a brighter workspace, where I could see the fabric so much better, and with the repetition of folding and pinning now familiar, the ironing under of the edges was soon completed.

Taking the fragrant, still-warm apron into the dining room where the light also streamed in from large windows, I sat on the floor beside my sewing box and threaded a new needle with muslin-colored thread. I leaned my back against the wall toward the kitchen, catching light from all my windows, and slipping my comfortable old thimble onto my index finger, began to sew the first apron.

Before the sun was halfway round the house, the hemming was finished. I cut out the neck and waist ties and decided to leave the ironing, hemming, and attachment of those until tomorrow. With enough light left of the day, I cut out two more aprons and ties. Time had passed quickly, and my stiff limbs and sore fingers confirmed that I had spent most of the day on just this first piece! Would it be worth these hours? I certainly needed to increase production if I was to profit from such an endeavor! But I did have to admit I found the time spent rewarding and even found myself humming from time to time. Certainly Solange would smile when I wrote to her of my sewing project.

Ten days had passed since Henri left the cloth in my arms. I knew he would pass again in another two or three. Did he really anticipate that I would have five aprons finished for him to take and sell? Stubborn as I was and working several hours each day, I completed each new apron in much less time than the one before and had finished all five. Of course I did! The first and most poorly put together apron would be mine. Henri could take the other four and do as he pleased.

Nearly ten meters of muslin remained, but I packed up the sewing box, not wanting to begin more. What if they didn't sell? As a last thought, I had put a deep pocket onto the front of the five finished aprons. Surely these deep pockets would be a benefit to any woman as they always were to me.

As expected, Henri arrived two days later with talk of his latest acquisitions and what he had sold and to whom. I stood with him at the road and listened with few comments, waiting for him to mention the aprons, which he did not do. We exchanged eggs for goods and still he had not asked. I realized he was waiting for me broach the topic, and he would but wait. When he made as if to leave, I finally told him I had four aprons he could take and attempt to sell. I was wearing the first I had made, as I am sure he noticed immediately upon his arrival.

"Oh good, Mademoiselle! Are they identical to the one you are wearing?"

I smoothed the front of my apron with my hands. "Yes, but the other four are better made."

"Turn around and let me have a look," he said, twirling his fingers in the air as a cue for me to do the same. "Yes, they will do fine. Very fine, Mademoiselle Marie!"

I raced to the house, returned with the four aprons neatly folded one on top of the other, and quite ceremoniously laid them into Henri's arms. "Do you really think anyone will buy them?"

"*Mais oui!* For I have already sold ten more. Sight unseen but greatly anticipated!" he said with dancing eyes.

With this last remark, he turned toward the open end of the wagon, gently placed the finished aprons into a box, and turned back round, producing a large stack of cut cotton swatches of various colors and sizes in many different prints. Folded like pieces of patchwork squares for quilts, the thick bundle was tied with twine and, like the bolt of cloth, was heavier than I anticipated.

"Many of the ladies requested a little color and adornment to their aprons. Your perfectly placed pockets would suit well for a little color, no?" And with that he was off once again. My aprons already sold and ten more to be made!

Next day and chores completed, the afternoon found me once again on the floor in my dining room beside the windows, untying the twine to set loose the stack of fabric patches. Most were folded into fours stacked again and again one on the other. As I unfolded them, I noted their differing sizes, some square, others rectangular, measuring an eighth to a quarter of a meter, making them large enough for a separate bodice. The smaller pieces were certainly adequate for roomy pockets. The fabric was all unused and obviously remnants from a dressmaker's cuttings.

Close to the bottom of the pile, I found the largest piece of folded fabric, measuring almost two meters. It was an attractive pattern of delicate flowers in a vibrant shade of lavender. Unfolding it over and over, I laid it out on the floor in front of me. Surely enough for a simple dress.

CHAPTER 14

THE POMEGRANATE, WINTER 1921

Everything about Henri was worn and dusty. His flopped hat, brown-hued pants, and ever-worn jacket of indeterminate cloth must have covered him for many years as he traveled up and down these roads. His creaky wooden wagon seemed an extension of his being with its metal, rust-crusted hinges that loudly announced the opening of the wagon's rear portal to reveal hidden wares on offer for the discriminate buyer. And Donkey, with no other name I knew or ever heard uttered by Henri, was of an indeterminate age as well. With his left eye glazed over and most likely unseeing and both his long ears notched and scarred, Donkey looked as though he had participated in fierce battles. How long had these two warriors of traveling commerce been together?

Now if I allowed myself, Henri's singing as he rolled along the road from the north to my house could possibly make me smile. He was such a constant and possibly reliable friend. Other than my infrequent trips to town, he was my only contact with places beyond my own. On this particular day, I was hoping to find sugar in his wagon.

Donkey greeted me with a turn of his head in my direction and graciously accepted my scratches and hugs to his warm neck. Henri watched us as he descended without a greeting and moved with seeming intent to the rear of the wagon. In one swift movement, he swung open the door and laid it flat, ready to place on it what he believed I desperately needed.

This day he put but one item in the middle of this space: a large, ripe pomegranate. One of the largest I had ever seen, its skin deep red and glossy. Henri looked from this fruit to my face. He was quite serious. Even his eyes that smile when all else is contemplative were dark.

"Mademoiselle Marie, how are we today?" he asked.

"We are well," I replied, looking from the pomegranate to him and back to the fruit again.

"Mon Dieu! Our winter is cold this year. How are your little hens doing in this air?"

I handed him my basket of two dozen brown eggs. "The cold certainly doesn't seem to affect their laying."

"Fine, fine," he said impatiently, putting the basket in the dark hold of the wagon as though the eggs were beside the point.

Although I was ever curious, I never asked Henri how far he traveled north and south on this road, what towns he visited, or where he acquired his goods. He was a peddler, a gypsy man I assumed, and when I did once ask how long he had been in commerce, his eyes smiled, and he responded, "It is the donkey that is in commerce. He just brings me along." I had not asked further. If he were so inclined, I imagined he would have many, many tales to tell.

Henri seemed as private a person as I and yet also my friend, and sometimes, I sensed, my benevolent protector. Although we were not related in any way by a shared past or common peoples, we seemed connected closely during his visits. He was solicitous and seemed genuinely concerned for my well-being. That must have been his nature with everyone, I thought, otherwise his caring regard on my behalf would have been a puzzlement.

Turning my attention to the pomegranate atop the wagon lid, he asked, "Do you know what lies here before you, Mademoiselle Marie?"

"Yes, I do," I told him.

"So you are familiar with this most exotic of fruit?"

"My papa would sometimes bring them home from his travels, and Solange would place them in a large bowl in the middle of our dining table."

"Did your papa explain that the pomegranate is feminine in form and nature?"

I certainly could not imagine Papa assigning gender to a fruit, and perhaps the look on my face said as much because Henri continued on, "Do you not see your image here before you? Lovely in color and design? The skin reflects the light and is not so tender as the color would suggest, but tough enough to protect what lies inside." His eyes focused only on the pomegranate. "In such a healthy fruit, as you see here, you can determine that below this covering of skin is life, rich red and waiting to burst forth. With color, color! The heart of the feminine, full to overflowing!"

I had never heard such words from Henri and certainly never amassed in such excited allegory. I stared intently at the fruit.

Henri stopped, sighed, and lowered his head. Had he known such a woman? Loved such a woman? He always had a tale to tell about each of his wares presented to me but never with such passion bordering on an intimacy that convinced us both to avoid each other's gaze.

Henri seemed in no hurry to resume his treatise and certainly neither did I. His purpose I could only ponder as we stood in the all-but-forgotten cold of the day. But purpose he always had.

He began again, talking quietly now. "This fruit is full because it was well tended. Otherwise, would it not be thin and dry of skin and heart?" He paused for a reply, but I stayed silent. "However, I bring today for you another as well. It still needs tending with sun and time. Then it too will become full. In time its color will also reflect health from skin to heart." And with that Henri pulled from the back of his ancient wagon another pomegranate, just as large as the first, but this one hard and unripe, perhaps plucked or fallen early from the branch. The skin was still mostly green with blushes of red color just beginning to move across its flesh. A fruit for another season.

He handed it to me and, looking into my eyes, said, "This one is for you, Mademoiselle. You have time to tend again." He placed it with great care into my hands as though it were precious, delicate, and fragile.

He began to close up his wagon, saying, "I leave now and will be two days south and then will pass by again in four days. By then you may have need of more than I can offer today."

He turned and began walking down the road beside Donkey, leading the wagon forward on foot, never glancing back. I stood there holding the unripe pomegranate. I had forgotten to ask about the sugar but wouldn't have even had I remembered. I did not think his stopping today was to sell but to offer, for whatever reason, this fruit that lay cold and heavy in my hands. I watched until he and Donkey were little more than figments in my mind.

I learned of Henri, the man, through the tales he told of all things he presented for sale or barter. Every pot, utensil, strip of cloth, and cutting of cheese came with a story. Not just a story but a sage tale woven of life's sinew. Did Henri talk such tales with each wagon stop? With each household along his way? He must have known every family and their tales as well. I shared no day-to-day stories with Henri for there was little to tell, but instead eagerly listened and welcomed his voice, as it was so often the only other one I heard outside of mine in my own head.

I turned and walked into my house. A pomegranate. What was I to do with this? And what was I to do with Henri's tale? The late afternoon sun filled the sitting room with light. I placed the fruit in the middle of the table not far from the window's warm pane. It looked forlorn. I took a piece of colored scrap, a bright crimson red, thinking it might encourage the ripening, and laid it beneath the fruit. Slowly, I paced back and forth from the kitchen through the front rooms and back again, thinking on Henri's strange words and looking at this odd addition to my space, hoping it would somehow thrive. It would remain here in this room in the sun's warmth where it might have the opportunity to truly ripen. It was all the tending I knew to give.

CHAPTER 15

THE BEEHIVES, LATE SPRING 1922

As spring gave way to summer, the house was far too stuffy and the warm air outside too inviting not to take my stitching to the river. My aprons were selling well, and I spent some hours of most days attempting to keep ahead of the growing number of requests for my work. I took pride in the fact that I was employed in useful labor from which I profited, which in turn allowed me to become even less dependent on Papa's generosity.

I closed the front door behind me, a blanket tucked under one arm, and had just bent my head down to check my basket for all needed sewing items when I caught a glimpse of movement to my right—out in my lavender fields just south of where I was standing.

I looked again, shading my eyes from the sun, and saw with some surprise Henri standing in the fields and gesturing with wide-flung arms, as if to encompass all the land visible. He was fiercely animated in what appeared to be a one-sided conversation with a nun who was running her hands through the lavender stalks and nodding at whatever he was imparting. I still had never been to the convent and had met none of the Sisters residing there, but I assumed this was one of them now standing in my fields with Henri. But why in the world were they here?

As I stood watching in the shadow of the stoop, Henri stepped off to the side, revealing four stacks of wooden boxes, three to a stack. Beehive boxes? Old and worn, they sat almost hidden among the tall stalks, sending the ever-present bees fleeing from the now tamped down area.

I knew the Sisters were beekeepers and then I realized what was happening, the scheme Henri was now concocting for my "benefit." Of course! Beehives in my fields! Was I now expected to tend and nurture bees, promoting the making of honey? Lavender honey? Had I not thought this myself, that lavender nectar from these bees would be divine? Never had I entertained the thought of actual hives in my fields; however, I did often wonder to where the thousands of noisy, buzzing bees flew to deposit their gatherings and create their honey.

I was unaccustomed to seeing anyone standing in the middle of one of my lavender fields, much less a nun from the convent. I stood still and watched the two. What was I to do? I remained just outside the door on the porch, hidden from their view as they were consumed in their conversation. Taking a deep breath (or was it a sigh?) I stepped forward, knowing Henri had been expecting me to appear.

With his arms still in flight over the fields, Henri motioned me over. I had never seen him so excited. I glanced back at the road, and there was Henri's wagon with Donkey at its head. Donkey was intently watching Henri as well. Perhaps he had never seen his master demonstrate such animation either! Henri was persuading, selling, coaxing, and I was suddenly embarrassed that he would, without even consulting me, think of offering use of my land to a stranger. I left the porch, and as I approached, I felt the rise of anger.

"Ah, Mademoiselle Marie! This is Sister Agnès, the prioress from our convent near Verdun. Now that our brave boys are home or gone from us, the Sisters are able to take up their former tasks once again. Life resumes its path, no?"

So this was one of the Sisters who also cared for the soldiers and who had found the family of my two boys. I eased at this recognition and also with the calming effect of her demeanor. She exuded respectfulness and reassurance. I realized that this idea had not originated with her, but she had been willing to come with Henri to see what plan he was devising. I felt she knew him as well as I did.

Sister Agnès met my eyes with a slight smile and what I perceived to be a shared empathy, as if to say, "Yes, our friend here is sometimes forward but only with the best of intentions." I looked for any sign of pity in her eyes but saw only a pleasant woman with a patient manner and sensed she understood my confused and flustered state.

"Let me explain, Mademoiselle Marie," Sister Agnès began. "We at the convent, the other Sisters and myself, are apiarists, beekeepers. We have maintained a small, thriving business producing honey and wax for candles. Henri has, for some time, carted our wares to customers and markets north and south of Verdun. People seem more eager than ever to sweeten their lives now that life has begun again. We believe the demand for our honey will grow faster than our limited hives can produce. Henri has told me many times that your fields of lavender are alive and vibrant with bees. He finally persuaded me to come have a look and a talk with you." Sister Agnès again looked into my eyes with an understanding that this was an awkward first encounter for both of us.

I nodded. Henri should have brought her first to my door, approached me first to talk of this. But, of course, Henri knew what I would have said.

He was searching my face, I knew, hoping to find my countenance restored to a modicum of calm, indicating a willingness to listen further. I did not avert my gaze from Sister Agnès. I was not yet relaxed enough to trust whatever words I might speak to him.

Seeing my hesitation, Henri seized his opportunity. "I have been describing to the Sisters for some time the expanse of your lavender fields and how your abundance of bees is a most excellent opportunity for making even more exquisite honey. So Sister Agnès and I, with your assumed permission, of course, Mademoiselle Marie, brought twelve hives today. Just as an experiment, to be sure, to see if your lively bees might take to a home close to their favorite nectar. And if so, then voilà! You and Sister Agnès can strike a bargain on purchasing your combs, the Sisters will produce their honey to sell, and everyone makes a fine profit."

Henri was aware that I was overwhelmed. He knew I was caught by surprise just as he understood I never would have agreed to the hives had he spoken to me ahead of time. He also knew I was polite and would not want to appear disrespectful to the nun, that my need for propriety superseded my distress regarding his presumptuousness and would cause me to hold my tongue. Once again he interrupted these thoughts.

"The bees will be no trouble to you, Mademoiselle Marie. The hives merely serve as an abode for your bees and a storehouse for their endeavors for which the Sisters will pay you a fair price. Am I not right, Sister Agnès?"

The Sister's kind eyes looked at me again, and in a gentle voice, she asked, "Have you ever tasted lavender honey?"

"No," I told her, "but I have often imagined it would be delicious."

She laughed quietly and said, "I want to be there when you have the first taste of your honey. It will not disappoint you. Should the bees take to the hives and should you consent to engage with us, there will be honey to overflowing. The hives brought today have been cleaned and prepared for new colonies, and we should know in a few weeks if your bees find them to their liking."

"But why here?" I asked.

"Your property is wide-reaching and the lavender very healthy. Your fields are more alive with bees than any I have seen over many years. Although we have active colonies at the convent, we have no hives dedicated to producing nectar from lavender alone, as your bees would do here. Truly I hope that if the bees lodge in these hives, we might come to an agreement. And, yes, the lavender honey will be delicious." As she said these last words, a broad smile of anticipated delight spread across her face just as my mouth began to water.

Henri interjected, "And the beauty is, Mademoiselle Marie: no trouble for you! I can bring Sister Agnès again in two weeks to inspect the work of our busy friends. A good plan, no?"

We were standing among hectares of early-blooming, fragrant flowers inhabited by throngs of bees, thousands upon thousands of them, the air alive with their movement and humming. I watched them for a moment alight on one bloom and then on to the next. Twelve hives. How many of them could live in twelve hives? I realized I was already licking the honey from a comb that could be created here in my rows.

"Would we really know in just two weeks if the bees take to the hives?" I asked.

Looking over the fields, Sister Agnès replied, "Perhaps not as soon as two, but certainly by three or four. I would suggest we assess how things are getting along in three weeks."

"All right, let's proceed," I said, looking only at Sister Agnès. "But I want to be involved every step of the way," I added emphatically.

I knew nothing about bees, hives, or honey making, but I knew my land and my lavender, and my bees had become a constant reminder of life moving round me. I found myself excited about this possible collaboration.

Henri assured us both again that this would be a great success. His role, in addition to bringing Sister Agnès out for inspections, would be to transport the combs from my house to the convent where the honey and wax would be extracted.

"And, Henri," I asked, finally looking at him, "what exactly will you gain from this enterprise?"

"Well, of course," Henri concluded earnestly, "I will add the lavender honey to the other honey and beeswax candles already sold to customers far and wide. We all will benefit." His sun-worn face lifted into a glowing smile.

Despite my excitement, I was still extremely exasperated with Henri but stubborn enough not to show any sign of frustration. Surely he realized that bringing the hives to my land without my consent was overstepping the bounds of appropriate intercession on my behalf? Yes, his ideas and schemes always seemed, one by one, to push me to take another step forward in life, but that in no way ever diminished my desire to want to chastise him severely for these intrusions into my affairs.

As we walked back toward the road and the waiting wagon, I asked Sister Agnès to explain how the bees might want to make a home in these hives. She said the hives they brought to my field were Langstroth hives and that several brood combs had been placed in them. The hope was that nurse bees would nurture the larvae and create a new queen, and the hives would then become active.

"Sister, I meant it when I said I want to be involved in all of it," I said, grasping both her hands in mine. "I want to learn about my bees, about the making of the honey. That must be part of our agreement."

"Of course, Mademoiselle Marie," she said while squeezing my hands. "The Sisters and I would like nothing more than to have someone new to teach. We become a little tired of ourselves," she said with a laugh, "and having a new friend to learn what we love would bring us great pleasure.

"If the hives are productive, we will talk together of adding more to your fields, and we will certainly need all the help you can provide. With your permission, *ma chère*, I will return in three weeks' time. Until then, keep watch on the hives from a distance, and perhaps you will see them begin to inspect their new homes. Hopefully they will find them to their liking. When we look together more closely, we can begin our planning and your education." With a smile, she placed a hand on my arm and turned to walk back to Henri's wagon.

I still did not meet Henri's gaze as he whispered a soft adieu in my direction. Whether this was a fine idea or not—and that remained to be seen—I was not going to relieve him so easily of any guilt that might twinge across his mind over his impertinence.

Looking back at the hives, the bees were, as always at this time of year, everywhere one could see. I would certainly keep a keen watch. As Henri assisted Sister Agnès onto the wagon seat, I couldn't help but think he was like Donkey, pulling a wagonload of potential on down a road to possibility.

CHAPTER 16

THE OTHER SISTERS, MAY 1922 – SEPTEMBER 1922

The bees quickly took to their new home in my lavender fields. When Sister Agnès, accompanied once again by Henri, came to visit the hives three weeks later, she announced with certain excitement that there was good evidence the bees were "settling in nicely." I felt Henri wanting me to meet his gaze but I was not ready for his gloating glare. Although I had seen him twice travel past my home during these three weeks, we merely waved to each other. I know he realized I was still upset with his insolence, and he did not wish a confrontation. My pride might have caused me to sabotage this scheme of his, and truly, I did not want that either.

I was excited and glad that the bees were finding my lavender a worthy home and felt a growing kinship with them. During those weeks of waiting I had watched the activities of the bees closely. First, I silently observed from the side of the house, and then gradually, as I saw them flying in and out of the new hives, I found myself moving closer. I also heard myself humming along with their grand buzzing and discovered they did not seem to mind my presence. I did not venture close enough to the structures to peer inside but kept a ways back, where the number of bees flying furiously to and from the boxes were fewer. The constant drone of their activity, however, reverberated as soon as I stepped outside my house. They were comfortable companions and I was grateful for their music.

Sister Agnès came with Henri twice again in May. Sometimes I would see Henri between those visits, and he and I would always walk out to the fields to check on the bees. Pride set aside and our mutual goodwill restored, our forays into my fields were pleasant and filled with expectation. He would venture close to the hives, seeming very much at ease with them. When I asked if he was ever afraid of being stung, he laughed and said, "I have been stung so many times I no longer feel their barbs to my skin. I have helped the Sisters for several seasons now as they harvest the combs."

At the end of May, Henri and Sister Agnès brought nine more hives, and the good nun also carried under her arm three wide-brimmed hats with long netting attached all around that would reach nearly down to our knees. Since the hives had arrived, I had taken to wearing long-sleeved blouses and a pair of trousers that fit me amazingly well, courtesy of Henri. I wondered what man had worn them before me. I intended to ask Henri to find me another pair, as I was finding them extremely comfortable and wore them most every day. Dressed in our bee clothes, we completed a thorough inspection of the thriving hives to the south and then placed the nine new hives in the fields to the back of the house. Sister Agnès was very confident that, just as with the first hives, more bees would quickly take up residence. More bees, more honey, and more music!

At the beginning of June, Sister Agnès invited me to the convent to begin my "education in apiculture," and so the following week, Horse and I drove our buckboard wagon the almost-hour north on the road toward Verdun, to the convent. The day was warm and clear. It felt adventurous to be on my own with my conveyance of horse and wagon, setting off for somewhere I had never been. Other than the infrequent trips to town for goods and food, there had been no reason for me to take any other excursions, and I truly welcomed the sense of freedom and change from my routines as Horse meandered down the road.

Upon my arrival, the Sisters were so welcoming of me that at first I was overwhelmed by their enthusiasm. I was not surprised, though, as I felt we knew much of one another through the caring of the soldiers and this new endeavor with the bees. Henri would certainly have communicated to them something of my past and current situation.

My first visit to their home began with a walk round all the buildings and grounds comprising the convent: their residence; a few outbuildings, including a long, narrow, somewhat crooked and worn-down shed; the herb, vegetable, and flower gardens; and the honey house. They saved the honey house for last. Inside it were all the components and equipment needed for harvesting and processing the honey and beeswax. It was difficult to take in all the information in one fell swoop. The Sisters used terms completely foreign to me, describing processes and demonstrating interesting contraptions, often talking over one another and sounding much to my ears like the humming of the bees in my fields. Moving back outside again, and gazing round their grounds, I asked if they kept chickens.

"Why would we do that, Marie, when Henri brings us fresh eggs from yours?" Sister Béatrice replied with a gleam in her eye.

I certainly knew I kept Henri well supplied with eggs, and I was so happy to know that they arrived here and were actually eaten. I sometimes suspected that Henri took my eggs and aprons and never really sold them. I was further gratified, and rather proud, when Sister Jeanne, resident cook for the convent, told me later that afternoon over tea how much she liked my aprons, especially the ones with the deep pockets. As I studied her features, I tried and failed to find some resemblance between her and my lost nurse-friend Jeanne. Finding none, I felt a sense of relief.

As the Sisters and I spent ever more time together, our previously unspoken curiosities about one another began to find voices as we, at first cautiously and later more comfortably, questioned one another about the small and few things we might have in common. They seemed to welcome, as did I, someone besides themselves to talk with. I certainly had done quite enough talking with myself and relished the possibility of women friends again.

And what were the topics of these first conversations? Certainly Henri was a common subject to us! As we exchanged stories and anecdotes concerning his involvement in our lives, we realized this man had affected us all and in ways that both amused and astounded. The Sisters unanimously agreed he was "a godsend" and assailed me with examples of how after the war he appeared and found for them provisions when so few were to be had.

"We were forced to flee Paris quickly when the war marched ever closer. We had to seek safety in Belgium, and taking our apiary equipment with us was never a possibility," said Sister Agnès. "When it was safe to return to France, the bishop found this piece of land. A small farm in great need of repairs but generously donated by the elderly landowner."

With deep gratitude, they were ready again to take up their cloistered life and their business with the bees. Henri procured for them much of the equipment, including the hives and extractor that they needed to start anew. They, in turn, supplied Henri with honey, wax, and candles that he sold locally and even shipped to customers farther away. I shared with them similar accounts of Henri's coming to my aid and somewhat but not completely, and certainly not as readily, agreed that he was a godsend.

These stories of our mutual friend and benefactor allowed us time to take our measure of one another and mingled with the opportunity to find cause for laughter. In doing so, we found an easy and companionable flow of give and take in our conversations. They inquired whether I would be offended if they asked me personal questions, admitting that they had long been curious about what had brought me to my house in Meuse.

I felt a letting down of defenses, shocked that I was now ready and willing to open up to these women whom I found kind and gracious. I felt a need to release some of what bound me so tightly—a desire to be more at ease with living, as I found them to be. I inhaled deeply and told them they could ask me whatever they wanted.

Their first question surprised me. I had expected them to ask something personal regarding my experiences in the war, and mentally and emotionally prepared myself for what might prove difficult to answer. But instead, they asked if I was ever afraid of living alone in my house on the river.

"Every day I am thankful to my maman for leaving me a serene place of refuge," I began. "On first arriving, the emptiness of the old house mirrored my own feelings, and I immediately felt its willingness to take me in with no expectations. It had sat empty and aging long before I arrived and was content to continue in the same state, only now with an injured soul within its walls. It has been my sanctuary as much as I imagine your convent is to you."

There were six Sisters at the convent, and none had ever lived alone and could not imagine being happy doing so. They had lived together at the current site since November of 1919 and were extremely thankful for the donated property so suited to their purposes.

Sister Agnès expressed the fear they felt as the war had moved relentlessly toward them, forcing their move from Paris to Belgium, and then again with the beginnings of persecution in that country. "Yet throughout those experiences we have remained together in one place or another, just as we have for the last twenty years." Together, the six of them, despite the hardships of those war years and after, and strengthened by their solidarity and faith, remained determined to return to France and reestablish their convent. Restoring the small depleted farm back to life had helped restore their own lives.

I found myself with tear-filled eyes, nodding occasionally as they spoke, but I chose not to share my own experiences during those same years of hardship. I supposed they knew I had been a battlefield nurse, and because of my training and experience they had Henri approach me on their behalf to take into my home and nurse the three boys. I did not know if Henri had chosen to share with them the state in which he had found me when I first arrived in Meuse. I thought not. I did know that they were appreciative of the care I provided to the soldiers when they had no room for more at the small convent.

Walking together over their grounds, we were silent for some time, all of us contemplating the memories of that horrid time of war. We were all, I thought, ready to move forward and create new experiences. I felt welcomed and so grateful to be offered a place beside them.

In all the many hours I spent with the Sisters, working with the honey and beeswax and enjoying a close friendship with them, talk of religion was never a conversational destination. I had never discussed my ambiguous Jewish heritage, and they did not discuss their faith with me. It was obvious they were devout, and their faith was in evidence in all they did.

Early on, they shared they had all left the homes of their parents between the ages of sixteen and eighteen, moved into the family of the Church, and had been with other Sisters of their order since that time. Other than their work in the gardens and with the bees, their routines centered on their prayers and chapel rituals, which to me were somewhat mystical and fascinating. They seemed to hold la Vierge Marie, the Virgin Mary, in high esteem, their devotion expressed in the few pictures in the convent chapel and in their frequent references to her in everyday conversation. It was as though she were real to them. So real, in fact, that I often thought of Mary as another Sister. Unseen in the physical but just as present.

Papa always made a point of instilling in Solange and me a cautious attitude toward any outward display of religion. Finally after years of relentless asking, and when it was just the three of us at home on a Friday, we would sometimes observe a loosely structured Sabbath together in the privacy of our home. If Papa was to host a dinner on a Friday, however, it was understood that no mention of Sabbath was ever to be spoken. We knew many of the men who attended our dinners were also Jewish, and conversations both lively and serious were enjoyed. But talk of religion, never.

Papa said we knew who we were and that was all that mattered. "Be wise and never add fuel to the fires of others' religious righteousness," he instructed us. Growing up I felt we three alone shared a well-kept secret. With the passing of my years, I have often thought that Papa was wise to be guarded. Even during the time after the war, there were stirrings of religious persecution, and I too felt guarded whenever discussing any religious aspect of life. And, truth be told, I held little now in the way of faith—neither in my heart nor in my head. During that time of nursing in those killing fields, I was always just a prayer and a blasphemous curse away from God, accusing Him daily of abandoning His own creation. The Sisters, in contrast, seemed to wear their faith as a comforting mantle. It was never solemn, dark, or secret. They seemed to harbor no anger at their God but only relief that He spared them from what could have been.

Over time, they each came to share with me their own personal stories of the circumstances surrounding the decisions for them to become nuns. Sisters Marguerite and Jeanne both came from very large, impoverished families, and their parents made a decision early in their lives to "give" a daughter to the Church. They were brought up knowing from a young age this was their destiny but certainly never had a clear idea of the reality. They accepted the idealistic visions of devotion and piety fueled by their family and their church.

Sister Evangeline said she easily and gratefully accepted her calling, as she wanted to please her parents and soften the financial burden of having three daughters and no sons. I came to think of Sister Evangeline as the Garden Sister, for she spent every moment apart from her religious duties out of doors in the gardens and dirt. She was never still and never happier than with a spade or rake in her hands.

Sister Béatrice, who never minced her words and could always provoke a laugh with her caustic humor and honesty, told me: "From my earliest memories, I watched three generations of men beat and belittle the girls and women in our family. I had no reason to stay and every reason to leave. I had no use for men then and life has done little since to change my mind."

Sister Dominique confessed she cried for months upon arriving at the convent as a young girl, and her superiors came close to sending her home—a place she did not want to go back to. As a girl, she had always wanted a husband and children and by the age of twelve had even chosen a local farm boy. But she knew once her parents sent her to the convent there was no going home to her family, as this would have been seen as a disgrace. The fear of her father's retribution soon dried her eyes. That, for me, explained her nurturing ways. She had found her family here, and she watched closely over the needs of her Sisters. She cared for the bruises, tended them when they were ill, made sure their garments were mended, and consulted with Jeanne on the weekly food plan and what stores were needed. She was especially devoted to Sister Agnès.

Sister Agnès was their prioress, the oldest sister of the convent, and truly the center round which their lives revolved. Sister Agnès listened at least twice as much as she ever spoke. In all the times with the nuns, I noticed that whenever one of them voiced an opinion, brought forth an idea, or expressed an emotion, Sister Agnès was always totally engaged. I wondered if this came with the responsibility for the care of her convent or if it was her innate nature. I came to know it was the latter. She reminded me of a calm, stately hen with her chicks. Sister Agnès always found ways to keep their minds sharp, bodies busy, conversations filled with laughter, and souls secure.

However, Sister Agnès did not share what circumstances brought her to a life in the Church. She seemed somehow above earthly considerations and, in my mind, was everything I imagined in a devoutly religious woman. Her perpetual smile reflected such a peace and harmony with all about her that I found myself wanting to always walk in her wake.

The women were so different of personality, yet their overriding sense of devotion and love for this family they had created was their common bond. They were not only Sisters in faith but friends who enjoyed one another's company. Their harmony with the life they had chosen and with one another extended toward me as well. I felt privileged to be so willingly included in their lives and their apiary work. They taught me as eagerly as I learned.

I remained curious in those first years of acquaintance as to what held them in that place and to a simple life so grounded in faith. They recited their daily devotion to la Vierge Marie, and prayers for her intercession for peace was their unremitting focus. All else they did, including their work with the bees and honey, were but secondary to their dedication to the Holy Mother.

I asked if they also revered the Pope, in Rome. They laughed and said, "Of course," but Mother Mary and Sister Agnès were their direct superiors, and it was obvious that was where their allegiance lay. They made me promise not to tell the Pope—or Sister Agnès! I loved their easy laughter; their way of looking at life seemed as simple as it was profound. I came to wonder if faith was the same as allegiance. If so, then my allegiance would fall always to Papa and Solange. And sometimes, perhaps, with Henri, if I were pushed on the matter.

My work with the Sisters in producing lavender honey and the beeswax candles fell into a comfortable pattern through late spring into late fall. Three days a week I would arrive at the convent at ten in the morning. I did not always need the wagon, especially once the combs were harvested, so just Horse and I made the trip. The Sisters would often be already at work when I arrived mid-morning, and I would seamlessly join in.

We would labor until one o'clock, then take a meal together at their kitchen's large round table, where sitting close together there was just room for us all. After, we would stroll about the grounds discussing the hives and our tasks yet to be done. We would end back at the honey house to finish our work. Often, when the weather of late spring, summer, and early fall was warm and inviting, we would move the long worktable out of doors into the shade of the honey house. There we would lick labels and stick them to the jars of fresh honey and boxes of candles. We sometimes ate our meal there as well. Regardless of the season, I would always allow two hours of last daylight for my return home, and smelling of honey, wax, and sweat, I would give Horse his head as we traveled back to my house on the river.

As late summer settled upon us, the harried work of bee season gradually slowed. My trips became weekly and then, by the beginning of September, settled into twice a month. With the gathering and processing of the honey mostly completed, the Sisters also traveled to the hives in my fields.

Two or three of us at a time worked together preparing the hives for winter. I learned that honeybees do not migrate or hibernate but stay active in their hives. They eat from the honeycombs, and their sole purpose is to keep the queen alive and warm. The Sisters taught me how to judge whether the hive was adequate for the size of the colony and had sufficient ventilation to ward against the wet climate, how to check the viability of the laying queen, and to make sure the bees had enough honey stores for their winter feeding. We removed vegetation from around the hives that might serve as a hiding place for small intruders and placed a grease patty of wintergreen in each to help limit the presence of mites during the cold months. I enthusiastically participated in these tasks and others as we spent many wonderful hours together in the lavender fields. It was another type of tending and helped ensure healthy hives come spring. Throughout the winter, I would check each of our hives weekly, adding more honey stores if needed and assuring all was well with my bees.

At the end of our afternoons of work at the convent, the Sisters never failed to invite me to afternoon vespers in their chapel, and I never failed to decline. While I accepted what they shared regarding their faith as their reality, and knew their devotion to be sincere, I never felt any desire or compulsion to join with them in any religious ritual. In turn, respectfully, they always made clear that it would never be a condition regarding our friendship. They ceaselessly extended upon me acts of kindness, and I was beyond grateful. I knew they came to truly love me as I did them. I would always take my leave with hugs all around.

As I traveled home, pleased with the work we accomplished and with a renewed sense of community, I was filled with their reflection of peace and contentment. Over the years, working side by side with these precious Sisters, a sense of peace and contentment gradually became my own reflection as well.

CHAPTER 17

FISHING, MAY 1922

Having dressed quickly for a day of chores in my comfortable pants and long flannel shirt, I stepped out the back door and secured three pieces of wood to awaken the barely glowing embers in my kitchen stove. With the fire flaring back to life, and while pushing sleep from my eyes and tugging my hair away from my face, I stepped out to the pump with my bucket. As I grasped the cold handle, the sound of Donkey's braying caught me completely unawares and quickened me fully awake. It was six in the morning. What was Henri doing here just after dawn? Walking round to the front of the house, Donkey, catching sight of me, let out another loud bray in greeting. Henri was nowhere in sight. Even this early, the morning's summer sun was beginning to warm Donkey's gray back. My cool hands welcomed his warmth as I nuzzled closer into his neck. "Where is your master, Donkey?"

As if on cue, Henri's rich voice broke into song. Donkey and I both looked toward the riverbank. My first thought was that Henri must be bathing and I needed to stay put. My second—that I had seen more than one naked man in my life and Henri would have to take his chances—got the better of me. With one last warm hug for my gentle friend, I walked across the narrow road onto the grassy slope down toward the river, following the music.

Henri was standing on the bank throwing a string back and forth across the glistening water. Small bugs hovering just at the surface scattered only momentarily as his line settled across the water in one long straight line. He was fishing!

I continued down the slightly sloped bank, approaching to his left. The new sun felt increasingly warm on my face. Walking up to Henri, I saw there were four fish on the bank, laid out neatly in a row.

With no apparent glance in my direction, he called a hearty, "Bonjour, Mademoiselle! Here we have a breakfast ready for cooking! One more tasty trout, then I fillet and we fry in cornmeal and have a feast!" A feast indeed! I had not had fresh fish since Marseille!

This late May morning was pristine; cloudless and still, the sun's rising sent bright rays between the poplars, illuminating all around in striations of light. My breath caught at the realization that in this moment I was grateful both of the company and the brilliant sun that was seeping into my senses.

"You, Mademoiselle, hold the line now and catch our last fish. I will begin to clean the others. My ravenous hunger will make my blade glide through these scaly beasts. Make certain this last one is long and fat!"

I still had not spoken. As I held the moment, I wondered if I was truly awake. I took the line from Henri, wrapped it round and round my hand, and, as he had done, held it still over the water. Henri hummed as he cleaned the fish, and I had become lost in the river's mesmerizing flow when I felt a strong tug on the line.

Struggling to keep the line secured round my hand, I hollered, "Henri! What do I do now?"

"Pull slowly and continue wrapping the string around your hand. Hold it taut! Any slack and our brave river beast will seize his chance to throw your hook!"

Our brave beast did indeed begin jumping high in the air for freedom. With each wild splash his scales caught the sun's rays. Again and again the fish jumped and twisted, tightening the line around my hand until it was biting sharply into my skin. I was not about to lose our breakfast, though, and continued winding the line steadily, moving the fish toward shore.

"*Bien*, Mademoiselle!" Henri yelled as the fish made one final leap and flopped to the shore beside my feet.

I had caught one! There were fish in my River Meuse! Breakfast, lunch, and dinner fish!

"Mademoiselle Marie, bring me your superb catch, and I will teach to you the fine art of filleting."

I bent down and grasped my sleek, speckled fish, but it flopped vigorously in my hand and I let out a loud gasp, dropping it.

"Ha ha! Your fish will be the most flavorful as it is the most lively. Use your two hands to scoop it up and toss it here."

I scooped and tossed as instructed, and Henri caught the slippery body with ease, as if it were dry. Joining him, I gathered his already-cut fillets and placed them into the fold of my flannel shirt. Within a minute, Henri finished the last two halves and added them to the others. He then pitched all the fish carcasses but that of my catch into the river.

"Look, Mademoiselle! Your fish was indeed full of life! She had many eggs inside her belly."

My heart sank at this news, and I felt a momentary pang of regret as we turned and walked back up the bank.

"Off to find skillets!" exclaimed Henri as he strode ahead with great purpose. "You do have two cast iron skillets, do you not, Mademoiselle Marie?"

Yes, they had been among the provisions he brought before the soldiers arrived, I reminded him. What I didn't say was that I had not used them since the boys had gone. Another pang at my heart. I picked up my pace to outdistance any pain and caught up to Henri.

"Did you build the fire up this morning? We need the stove hot for frying."

Glad I had stopped to refuel the kitchen stove, I assured Henri it would be ready for cooking breakfast. My mouth was beginning to water as my stomach rumbled, voicing its eagerness to eat.

"And, of course, we need four eggs from your coop and two potatoes, peeled and chopped. I brought the cornmeal and the cream for batter," he said as he sprinted to the wagon and I climbed the steps to my house to stir the fire.

It was then I realized that his fishing this morning had not been a spontaneous occurrence but a planned event. I felt the familiar twinge of caution and wondered what he was up to now.

Henri brought in the cream and cornmeal and placed them on the counter beside the waiting eggs. He grabbed a stone bowl from the open shelf and quickly cracked the eggs and added the cream, whipping them into a frenzy. I assumed he must have been fueled by a great hunger as well.

I found the long-abandoned cast iron skillets and surreptitiously wiped away the thin coat of rust with a rag. After tossing another piece of wood into the fire, I placed the skillets atop the stove and quickly peeled and chopped the potatoes.

"Your lard please, Mademoiselle Marie. Three tablespoons in each skillet," Henri directed. The lard crackled as it hit the bottom of the hot pans. When it was judged hot enough to fry, Henri told me to lay the diced potatoes evenly in one pan as he laid the battered and cornmeal-covered fish in the other. I was feasting on the aroma alone.

Glad now for the table and chairs to hold our bounty and make us comfortable while we ate, I hurried to clear it of my sewing paraphernalia. As I stepped back into the kitchen, Henri lifted out the first batch of fish: five golden-brown fillets. He set them on a cloth to drain and slid the last five into the skillet. He had stirred the potatoes and they were beginning to brown as well.

As I reached for two plates, Henri asked if I had wine goblets.

"No," I said and laughed. "Why ever would I have need of those?"

"Then any glasses will do, as I have also brought a bottle of white wine, a baguette, and an aged Brie de Meaux for dessert. Please take out the last of the fish and dish the potatoes, Mademoiselle, and I will return *immédiatement* to eat," he said as he hurried out the front door.

Hmm. Again I wondered why he had gone to such trouble—a breakfast of fish and wine!

After laying the last of the golden fillets on the draining cloth, I grabbed two forks, knives, and linen cloths for *serviettes* and set our places at the table. Back in the kitchen, I divided the potatoes onto our plates, then added five crisp fillets to each and all but ran to the table, ready to begin eating as soon as possible. In the doorway from the kitchen to the dining room, steaming plates in hand, I stopped in my tracks. Imagine my surprise! At each setting sat crystal goblets filled with a clear wine, and in the middle of the table Henri had placed the small round of Brie de Meaux and a fresh baguette. Where oh where did he find such treasures? It was a treat for the eyes as well as the palate.

Besides eating with my sister, this was the first meal in my home with a friend. Henri had never been inside my house other than when carrying up the beds, mattresses, linens, and the boys. He now seemed perfectly at ease and at home sitting there in the sun-filled room. Any qualms I had about this meal I laid aside, too hungry for cautious speculation.

As the fish approached our greedy mouths, Henri quickly thanked the brave beasts for their "noble sacrifice." Had I ever tasted food this delicious? Fish this succulent and *pommes frites* so perfectly crisp? It wasn't until we began to break the baguette that we uttered sounds other than those of communal delight. Our mutual "ahhhs" and "mmms" indicated we agreed our feast was *magnifique!*

With a second glass of wine, the Brie, and a peach produced from who knows where, I shared with Henri my memories of shopping for seafood in the fish markets along the wharf in Marseille. Solange especially loved octopus and would buy it fresh from the fishermen as they entered the harbor, before they even stepped ashore. She sliced it thin, sautéed the opaque pieces in hot olive oil, then drizzled them with lemon and salt. Solange only made the octopus when it was just the three of us, as she said it had to be eaten hot from the pan. When we had Papa's business guests over for dinner, she chose scallops and thick, succulent cuts of white fish. Henri listened attentively to my tales, asking few questions but obviously enjoying the stories. He said he had lived inland his whole life, always by the Meuse but never on the sea.

"Do you ever miss living by the sea? And your family home in Marseille?" he asked.

"This place provides me the sanctuary I have needed, and although I greatly miss my sister and papa, I have grown to love the peace here these last two years. This is truly my home now, and I have no urge to return either to the city or the sea." I paused a moment, reflecting. "I do love that the river running so near provides such calm and serenity. I have needed that, too."

Henri sighed deeply, looked down, and placed his hands on his lap. He then turned his head to the left and looked up and out the window.

"I knew your mother, Marie," he said quietly.

My mind took a moment to catch what I thought I had just heard. Henri knew my mother? I must have spoken this aloud, as he said, "Yes, I was acquainted with your mother's family for many years."

My hands had dropped lifelessly into my lap, the fish forgotten and the bread sitting large in my throat. I swallowed again and again to get it down as my heart raced and my mind filled with questions tumbling over the other. "How did you know her?" I finally asked.

Henri then turned back to face me and, after taking a long breath, said, "She was twelve when I first saw her. Older than me by two years. I have traveled these same roads since I was quite young. That summer, I was with my uncle."

Wanting to ask only about my mother but not knowing how, I said what sprang first to mind. "Where were your parents?"

"Oh, they were here, close by. My family was very large, with many uncles and cousins who farmed on small parcels of land around our village. Between planting and harvest time, we would traverse the roads, usually two men together, to the outlying villages selling and procuring goods we bought in the larger towns. That way the families were kept together by farming as well as by the business, which supplemented the meager incomes from our harvests. My father first took me on the roads with him when I was seven. But even at that age I was in conflict with him continually. As I grew into eight and nine years, we argued fiercely—about anything and everything. I always said I knew better and he always believed he knew best."

Henri stopped, wiped his mouth on the linen, and picked up his story again. "By my ninth year, my father relegated me to traveling with my uncle, who also had his own wagon and donkey. Father and I were both relieved at this new arrangement, and our relationship improved the less we saw of one another. My father would take his wagon south and Uncle had this northern route through Verdun. That is why I missed those earlier summers of seeing your mother.

"My uncle was Father's younger brother, but you would have thought them no relation. Uncle called himself 'Pedro,' which was a ridiculous name for a Jew. He said it sounded exotic. This was the only common opinion my father and I ever shared. I refused to call him anything but Uncle." Henri paused here, and I followed his movement as we both took a drink of wine.

"Uncle was full of mirth, friendly and, I often thought, too familiar with the customers. But he liked people and was interested in the lives of the families he sold to. My father was all seriousness. I realized much later that, being the eldest, he was perhaps never far from worry as he shouldered all the financial responsibility for the success or failure of the families." Henri stopped and sipped his wine. "But I have ventured away from the story of your maman," he said, looking at me directly for the first time since he started his tale.

"So the summer of my tenth year, as we approached this house, I saw your mother and your own uncle. Actually, I heard them laughing and singing before they came into view. This certainly caught our attention and my interest! The only person we ever sold to here before was an older woman, and I seldom took any notice of her.

"But these children were a different matter altogether. I wanted to jump from that bumpy wagon seat and ease my aching body and dust-filled eyes with the vision of them, and run and run as the girl was. As we drew closer, I saw that the boy was sitting on the ground laughing, but he joined in the song as the girl ran around and around him.

"Uncle called out a greeting and the children stopped their game and ran toward the road to await our wagon. He knew their names: Edith and Paul. The children called him Pedro. How I hated that name, but coming from them it seemed not half so bad. Uncle introduced us all, and while the boy appeared shy, the girl was lively and full of questions. Why was I with Pedro today? How old was I? Did I go to school? What did we have in the wagon that they might like?

"I had no answers for I had no thoughts. She filled all the air with her energy, and I could not breathe. She was darting about the wagon, and I wanted but to hold her in one place and put the pieces of her together.

"Her grandmother, your great-grandmother, came out of the house just then and joined us at the wagon. She and Uncle conducted their business as the three of us conducted our awkward first business as well. For is it not the business of children to engage in play and inquiry? We stood in front of the wagon as far from the adults as possible. Uncle always talked loudly, and when he was coaxing to sell, his voice took on a powerful timbre. He was in his element and was also a distraction as we three were attempting to scrutinize one another and manage our own coaxing toward possible friendship.

"Your mother and uncle were dressed in simple summer clothing. She wore a cotton dress etched with lavender flowers, with a ribbon tied at her waist and another holding her long honey-colored waves away from her face. Her skirt stopped just above her ankles, and although she was now standing still, the toes of her bare feet were curling and uncurling as though standing in place was indeed a most difficult task. Her eyes, so like yours, were never the same color, shifting through variations of blue, green, and gray. Over the next three years of summer visits, we came, I think, to know each other well. But what did that thirteen-year-old boy truly know other than the hope of desired friendship from someone so . . . alive?" He paused again and looked at me with something much like despair in his eyes.

"Our route took us north one week and then back south again the next, with several days between at home with our families. I lived for those stops at your great-grandmother's house. This house. Your home now. For your mother was always either out of doors or seemed to sense our coming—she was always waiting there at the front. Perhaps our stops provided her with needed diversion from those long summer days with only a somber younger brother and her grandmother for company. I dared not believe she looked forward to our stopping for my sake. She was all life and beauty, and I rode atop an old wagon pulled by an ancient donkey with my crazy uncle Pedro.

"The long span of those summer-to-fall months allowed me time to ever ponder the color of her eyes. Every spring I vowed that this summer would be the one when I would discern their true color and hold it fast in my mind's eye. Over three summers of peddling, as we stopped here for as long as I could stretch each time, I never did accomplish my goal.

"The next summer Edith came alone to visit your great-grandmother. The hard, cold weather of the previous winter had been too much for your delicate uncle Paul, and he passed just days into the new year. Your mother was quieter, but her bare toes still danced, and by the last days of August, just before they returned home to Belgium, she was almost again my joyful friend."

Henri gazed out the window and continued in a hushed voice that spoke of loss. "That was the last I saw her. Your great-grandmother continued for some years to come here, to her summer home, but Edith never visited again. I begged Uncle to ask the grandmother for information. He told me it was out of the question. That it was none of our business. This struck me at the time as ridiculous, as Uncle was ever curious about the comings and goings of everyone. I sensed he felt my loss as well. One summer, two years after Edith's last visit, as Uncle was closing the wagon, I found the courage to ask your great-grandmother after her. She remarked that her granddaughter was now a young woman, and that her attentions needed to be focused on her future—carefree summers were a thing of childhood and in the past. She seemed to be reciting what she had been told, and I knew she was lonely for her summer companion as well.

"When you told me this was your mother's home, I immediately knew you to be Edith's daughter. Your eyes, you know. And your chin, and your hair . . ." Henri looked to me now, and we both sat still, staring at each other across the table.

The sun had moved across the sky, the poplars now casting long shadows along the road. Hours had passed as Henri transported us back in time. We were both fatigued, he from the effort of talking and I from the mingled pain and joy of listening. I wanted details. To know her face, how her laugh sounded, the way she spoke and danced. I wanted to feel her arms around me. But details would have to wait. It had been a day of mixed and many blessings, and all I wanted now was to think alone on what Henri had found the courage to share.

As we cleared the table, I said, "You know, no pictures or resemblances of any kind exist of either my mother or Solange's. I have so often tried to conjure an image of her face in my mind. Henri, I so appreciate you sharing your recollections with me. I truly do." He lowered his eyes and nodded. There would be more opportunities to share once the talk of this day had settled in.

When Papa first told me about Maman's house in Meuse, he said that she had spent her childhood summers here with her grand-maman. As Henri set about to leave, he answered my last question of the day, confirming that although the house had been unoccupied for the last twenty years or more, he had kept watch on the property and often fished the river in the spring and summer as he did today. He checked for vagabonds and rodents, tending to the house as might be needed, sometimes sleeping in the lean-to if repairs took more than a day. I realized then why the house had seemed untouched by long years of emptiness. Even in my initial state of depression and grief during those early months, I had thought it remarkable that a house long abandoned had withstood the elements of weather and time so well. And now I understood the source of Henri's fathomless wellspring of kindness toward me.

In my daydreams I had thought of my mother here as a grown woman but never as a child. Why, I don't know, as she had married my father at the age of nineteen, and I was born one year later. It was in her early years of summers that this was her home. And then she was gone.

I wandered through my home those next few days trying to conjure visions of Maman, young Oncle Paul, and my *great-grand-mère* here at this same time of year. Outside, I could picture them running and singing as Henri had described: Maman in the flowered dress, laughing and singing among the lavender.

And Great-Grand-Mère. I sensed that I was perhaps more like her than my maman. I had a passionate nature, and when riled I could respond too quickly with a comment or word. At those times, and with some humor I did not always appreciate, Papa would tell me I reminded him of my great-grand-maman; that she too was "feisty." No one would have ever described me as "joyful," as Henri had described Maman. I had always sought solitude and peace, now more so than ever. There was happiness enough in that.

Sitting on my steps in the day's last light, watching the spring sun glide down behind the poplars into the river, I felt the presence of my family round me. Even during the terrible time of anguish toward healing, they had been part of the solace here in my house in Meuse. My maman had given me life again.

I sighed deeply, a smile coming to my lips, for when I looked down at my bare feet, my toes were dancing.

CHAPTER 18

PEDRO, THE LITTLE BEAST, SEPTEMBER 1922

The rain was falling fast and hard. The torrents of water on my roof obliterated the welcome braying of Donkey, and it wasn't until I heard Henri's loud calling of "Marie, Marie! It is wet out here! Come give me your eggs!" that I grabbed my basket, covered my head, and ran out my front door and down the steps to the wagon waiting in the road.

Henri wore a hooded oilskin poncho, and as the rain began to let up he allowed the hood to fall onto his back, his floppy hat still securely in place atop his head. He moved round to the back of his wagon swiftly, anticipating the clouds opening upon us again, and threw open its heavy door. I handed over my full basket of eggs and seven more aprons, and as he placed them deep into the wagon, away from the rain, a small animal emerged, crying loudly.

"Ah!" Henri exclaimed in surprise. "Not you once again, my little beast! How is it you always manage to find a ride?" The kitten was mewing loudly while his head nuzzled Henri's hand.

This "beast" was the smallest kitten I had ever seen. It was black with white paws too big for his scrawny self, and one ear was all white. The port at Marseille was home to throngs of stray animals and cats were constant citizens of the streets and markets, so I knew them well. Cats were the rat-eaters and kept the port's population of such rodents down to a manageable level, while all the while the good people of town pretended the rats were nonexistent. I had a visceral, intense dislike of rats and saw cats as a necessity to be tolerated.

"Yes, yes, little fellow. I will feed you momentarily," Henri said, handing me the now-purring kitten. "Please hold him, Marie, and I will find him some nourishment."

Taking the warm kitten, I gathered him to my chest to keep him at least partially dry from the sporadic fall of raindrops. He crawled upward and settled into the curve of my neck, purring more loudly. I felt instantly warmer. As Henri laid some small cut-up pieces of smoked fish out on the table of the wagon front, I attempted to place the kitten there as well to eat. But the little feline was having none of it, and his tiny sharp claws extended with my continued attempts to lift him from my neck. I gave up trying to coax him off me (the claws were quite a deterrent) and succumbed to his clinging to the fabric of my clothing as he settled once again into my neck, continuing his music of contentment. "Henri, can you please help dislodge your cat from me so he can eat?"

"He is not my cat, Marie. He is nothing but an escapee from his littermates. A smart one, he is, for he has done this before, knowing I will not let him starve, and thus he scampers up inside the wagon when I am loading or unloading. Just let him rest where he is. He must need your warmth more than my food."

Our long-familiar routine of acquiring my mail and weekly provisions from Henri continued. I appreciated the convenience of not having to drive Horse and the wagon too frequently to town, I preferred to support Henri's business, and, most importantly, it gave us cause to visit. Collecting my requested bread, tea, and sugar from the rear of the wagon, he carted the goods up the steps to my house and set them against the front door, out of the rain. He returned to where I stood with his contented cat and proceeded, with what seemed a hasty retreat, to jump aboard his wagon and make as though to depart.

I realized his intentions as he picked up Donkey's reins. "Henri, you are not leaving this cat with me! I am serious! Henri!"

"It is not I that am leaving the cat, Marie, but that the cat has decided to stay!" He lifted the poncho's hood back over his hat, ordered Donkey forward, and off they went. Without even leaving me the dried fish to feed the little rascal!

Oh well. It was not such trouble. I walked toward my house with the warm, sleeping kitten tucked deep into my neck. It would not wake or be woken even when I squatted to retrieve my food supplies from the porch. With one hand I held the kitten securely and with the other clutched my supplies, making two more trips to and from the door to transport everything inside. Again the kitten began to purr. I felt the sound resonate through my body and knew he was mine.

Pedro.

I would call my little beast Pedro.

CHAPTER 19

HEALING, LATE NOVEMBER 1922

I t was not yet light on a Monday morning when I heard loud knocking at my front door. This was the first knock upon my door since occupying my home, and it caused me to jump up and dash to the window to see who might be there.

It looked like Henri but not quite. What was he doing here this early and why the urgent knocking? I hastily wrapped a shawl over my nightdress and moved to unbolt and open the door.

"*Dieu merci*, Marie, that you are up and about! I apologize in the extreme that I must seek you out so early but am most glad you are available."

Henri held his hat before him in both hands, turning the edges of the brim round and round with his fingertips as he spoke. It was evident he was in great distress. My first thought was of Donkey. My second thought, having only seen Henri without his hat perched on his head once before, was how his dark hair was very thick and quite lovely. Long at the sides and tucked back behind his ears, the glossy dark waves rolling over his head, for whatever reason, had caught me by surprise. He looked almost young standing there in the pre-dawn light.

Bringing myself back to his urgency, I asked, "Has something happened to Donkey? Or you? What's wrong?"

"No, no, Donkey and I are well. It is Sister Agnès! I have hurried here from the convent to bring you to them. They bid you come quickly, as she is in great need of your assistance." Henri beckoned me toward Donkey and the wagon.

"What do you mean? What's happened to Sister Agnès?"

"She has fallen, with a great gash to her head. The Sisters have stopped the bleeding, but she has a wide wound and has not awoken from a long sleep. Please, Marie, let's go now. *Rapidement!*"

"Yes, yes. Give me just a few minutes to gather some things." I ran up the stairs and quickly changed into my trousers and warm flannel shirt, but things? What things would I gather, as I kept no true medical supplies in the house? Thinking as best I could at this early hour, I grabbed strips of muslin from a basket of material scraps. From my sewing box I snatched up my small scissors, three needles of different sizes, squares of clean cloth, and two spools of my heaviest thread. I threw them all into a canvas bag, wiggled into my cloak, and slammed the front door behind me.

Henri was already waiting with reins in hand and pulled me up beside him. As I sat down, I asked, "What do you mean she is sleeping?"

"I know no more than I have told you, I'm afraid. I have not seen the good Sister, as when I arrived at the convent, Sisters Dominique and Evangeline were waiting with this news and then rushed me off to fetch you."

During the ride to the convent, I wondered whether Sister Agnès had simply fallen and had resulting head trauma that caused, hopefully, just a temporary loss of consciousness or whether she had suffered a more serious event prior to the fall. In any case, I knew I could at least conduct an examination and suture the wound. Although my medical training and battlefield experience with trauma and injury would allow me to examine and treat her, I was not a physician, and skills much greater than mine might be needed.

"Why did you not go to the local physician the Sisters would normally call upon?"

"He left at the beginning of the war and has not returned. He was a single gentleman and joined the ranks of the medical corps early on. No one has had word from him—whether he survived and, if so, if he might return. Hence the need for your services."

"You do know that I am a nurse and not a physician."

"Why yes, of course! But you are an *experienced* nurse and a gifted healer. Did you not heal the boys and return them to their family? The Sisters said the last letter from their family joyously reports their continued improvement and is a testament to your skills!"

Inwardly, I groaned and feared another expectation, a greater expectation, was being placed on me once again. But at least in this situation I had the security of training, experience, and some success. I was terribly worried for our dear friend and knew I must, for the remainder of the bumpy ride, set my mind apart from my emotions, putting on my nurse's mantle in preparation to deal with her needs.

Henri and I rode the rest of the way with our own thoughts. As we approached the convent I shaded my eyes from the sun's rising and noted silhouettes of three Sisters appearing from yet a distance away. When we were within fifty meters, they began moving toward us with cries of, "Hurry, hurry!" and "*Merci mon Dieu!* You've come!"

I jumped from the wagon with my bag of hope and rushed past their confidence. They led me to Sister Agnès's room. I had not been there before but it appeared much the same as the other Sisters' rooms, small and spare, only this one faced the east. The morning sun streamed through the window beside the bed on which Sister Agnès lay. She was illuminated in this light, and I could not help attributing some meaning to her shining countenance. Whether a positive or worrisome portent, I could not yet know.

Sister Evangeline motioned me to the chair at the bedside, where she had been in constant attendance, she later told me. We were all silent, gathered round Sister Agnès for those first few moments after my arrival. My initial observations, as I saw her face sustained some color, allowed me to exhale with relief that she was not at death's door. Her chest rose and fell gently, and as I placed my index and middle fingers to her neck, I felt her pulse strong, if somewhat erratic. Turning next to examine her wound, I found the gash on the left side of her forehead was nearly two centimeters deep and five centimeters in length. It was red, raw, and gaping but clean, and the bleeding but an ooze. The

Sisters had certainly taken good care of their prioress and friend. I attempted to wake Sister Agnès with a gentle shake, calling her name quietly and then louder, with more fervent shaking and rubbing of her hands. No response.

"Please tell me what happened, how long ago, and what caused this gash to her head," I said gently to the other Sisters.

"Yesterday afternoon we decided to pull up the last of the dead vines and prepare the garden for winter. But it's been so dry and the ground was so hard Sister Agnès said we needed the shovel from the shed, as we couldn't pull the vines cleanly from the ground," Sister Evangeline explained. "I went on picking for some minutes and then stopped when I realized Sister Agnès had not yet returned with the shovel, and we had not much time before vespers. I wondered if the shovel had been misplaced and she couldn't find it. Had I maybe set it down somewhere out of sight?" Sister Evangeline paused and stilled herself before continuing.

"I decided to walk to the shed, thinking I could help her find it. I didn't see her when I first walked in. The tools are kept at the far end, and it was walking that way that I saw her in the shadows. She had fallen to the ground and lay on her left side, the injured side of her head on the dirt floor. She wasn't moving, and as I knelt beside her I saw the blood. It was still running onto the ground. I ran as fast as I could for help." Near tears and visibly shaken, Sister Evangeline paused once more. I rose and guided her gently by the elbow to the chair where she could sit and compose herself.

Sister Dominique picked up the story from there. "After initially trying to rouse her in the shed and finding we could not, we raised her between us and carried her back inside to her room. We cleaned the wound but found the bleeding difficult to stop, so we gathered clean cloths and folded them into thick pads, taking turns holding them firmly to her head. Eventually, the bleeding slowed and after an hour finally ceased. She did not seem to be in pain, as she made no sounds at all. She has been asleep since we found her on the shed floor."

"Can you estimate how much blood she might have lost? And would one of you please put a large kettle of water on to boil?" I felt the loss of blood must not have been too great. She continued to display good color, and other than not responding, her pulse remained strong. I needed to clean and sterilize the wound and suture it closed.

"Perhaps a quarter liter of blood was lost," Evangeline said with some doubt in her voice. "The blood on the ground in the shed and the blood from the soaked pads would indicate perhaps that or a little more."

Significant but not worrisome. What concerned me more was her continued unresponsiveness and the fact that she had now had no water or nourishment for more than fifteen hours. Suture first and deal with that after, I quickly decided.

I went with Sister Evangeline to the kitchen and scrubbed my hands. Sister Jeanne was taking care of cleaning the bandages they had used and had put a kettle on as I had asked. I poured a portion of the boiling water into another pot, which I set back on the stovetop. As it resumed boiling, I put my scissors and needles into the water and then asked for a small table to be placed beside the chair in Sister Agnès's room, and for Sister Dominique to scrub her hands also, as she would assist me.

I wrapped the boiled implements in a clean piece of muslin to dry and carried them back to Sister Agnès's room. Henri was standing just outside the bedroom door, his hat still in his hands. "Do you have a drink stronger than wine in your wagon? One with a very high alcohol content?" I asked him.

"I am sure I have something, but are you wise to take drink that strong before you begin to sew? Maybe just a little port to calm the nerves, Mademoiselle?"

I couldn't help but smile. "It isn't for me. I need it to sterilize the wound and perhaps provide a little sip for Sister Agnès if she awakens during the suturing."

He smiled in return and hurried to the wagon. I knew he would come back with what was needed. He always did.

I finished laying out my few implements on the muslin atop the side table as Henri walked into the room and handed me a small, much-worn stone jug. As I pulled out the cork with a *pop*, what was inside smelled very strong and very old. "What is it?" I asked, wrinkling my nose.

"I am not altogether sure, actually. It is from a local gentleman from whom

I purchase the tonic for other local gentlemen. Everyone assures me it is highly medicinal!"

"Yes, it smells like it will clean a wound quite well!" I responded with a smile as I threaded my needle and tied a secure knot at the end.

I settled onto the chair and held a small pad of cloth below the cut to catch the alcohol as it flowed into and out of the wound. With a clean cotton square, I patted the wound dry and proceeded to close the gash. Fifteen stitches later, and with more alcohol to finish, I let it dry, covered it with lavender salve and a clean bandage of muslin, and found myself sending a prayer to la Vierge Marie asking that the gash not become infected. Sister Agnès had not stirred during the time it took to make that straight seam of her flesh, and yet I felt there was some sense of awareness on her part. I would let her body settle from the stitching before examining her further and take this time to talk with the nuns regarding events of the day.

I gathered my tools into the muslin and left Sister Evangeline again at the bedside. The remaining five of us moved into the kitchen. A kettle was put on for tea, and we drank and munched some bread and honey as we talked through the incident.

Henri soon joined us and reported, "I went to the shed, and it appears the good Sister fell against a hatchet that was leaned among the assortment of other tools, head side down. The blood has soaked in and dried dark on the ground. The hatchet head is covered with dried blood as well. It is astounding that her injury was not greater—astounding that she is alive."

"It is not her time to be taken from us! Sister Agnès has had some experience with close calls of this sort, and we always attribute it to the fact that she has angels of protection," Sister Jeanne chimed in as she refilled our teacups.

"What other close calls do you mean?" I asked.

The Sisters began recounting stories of Sister Agnès's escapes from serious injury: multiple bee stings that would cause her eyes to swell shut and breathing to become shallow, days of vomiting from mushrooms she would "try first," measles and other illnesses of unknown origin.

"But no unexplained dizziness, previous falls, or injuries to her head?"

"No, none," they assured me.

We finished our tea and together went to check on our patient. Her limbs were completely flaccid, and she continued to be unresponsive to my voice calling her name or to my moving her arms and legs.

I wanted to see firsthand the site of her accident, so Henri accompanied me to the shed. The weathered outbuilding was long and narrow and tilted with age, bent to the shadows even in late morning. Nails studded the heavy wooden support beams along both the left and right walls. From one of the nails on the right there hung a thick jute rope, its length extended down the wooden wall with the end tamped into the dirt floor. I stopped and scuffed at it with my boot where it lay partially exposed in the dirt and uncovered the entire end of the rope—a tied loop that had lain in wait for the Sister's unsuspecting shoe, approximately a body length away from the far end of the shed where the tools leaned into the dark corner. The hatchet, crimson with stale dried blood, was still on the ground where Sister Agnès's head met its thick metal blade. Henri and I looked up at each other at the same time.

"I hate ropes," I said quietly.

"Mon Dieu!" he replied, slowly shaking his head. He put his hand gently on my arm, and we turned and walked back to the convent.

Henri and I shared with the others our theory that Sister Agnès's shoe had caught in the loop of the hidden rope, causing her to pitch forward, her head striking the hatchet blade as she fell to the ground. They all moved as one out to the shed to see this for themselves. That left Henri and me to sit with our patient.

"Henri," I started, "I want to stay here for the night. It concerns me that Sister Agnès has not yet woken, and I need to examine her closely when she does. She will also need water and whatever food she can take."

"Of course, Marie. I will remain as well. The Sisters will be reassured by your presence."

"I will keep the first watch from now till midnight and change off with the Sisters."

Henri simply nodded.

The Sisters returned from the shed and agreed with our conclusion regarding the cause of the fall as well as with our decision that Henri and I remain with them through the night. We assigned shifts to watch over our prioress. I knew these next few hours were crucial, and even when encouraged to get some sleep, I was determined to remain awake and with her at least until midnight.

The nuns retired to their respective rooms, and I settled in for my watch. At his insistence, Henri brought blankets from his wagon and slept on the floor outside Sister Agnès's bedroom. By ten o'clock, I found myself barely able to keep my eyes open, my chin bobbing up and down and falling onto my chest. I began to hum to stay awake and then my fingers began to accompany my humming of "Für Elise," tapping out the notes softly on Sister Agnès's bed sheets. I found the humming helped keep me awake and I "played" several short pieces using her bed as my keyboard.

Suddenly, after my fourth rendition of "Für Elise," Sister Agnès opened her eyes, looked directly at me, and said, "I played that piece when I was a girl."

I was so surprised to hear her voice that I let out a small gasp of relief. She smiled softly and fell asleep again. I began gently shaking her arm. "Sister, Sister," I said as firmly as possible, "you need to stay awake! You need to drink some water and try to eat something. Sister Agnès, please try to open your eyes again!"

She once more looked at me, smiled ever so slightly, and returned to sleep yet again. At least I knew she could be roused. I was desperate to have her take some fluids, and as I propped up her head she managed to swallow reflexively a few sips of water. I was relieved when she didn't choke, and in my firm nurse's voice I told her she must take some more sips. Again, she was initially compliant and drank a little more before turning her head to the side in refusal.

This was encouraging progress, and although I wanted to share this good news with the others, I didn't want to disturb their sleep. And so I sat back again in my chair and knew that when it was my turn to sleep, I could do so with instructions for each bedside monitor to rouse Sister Agnès at least once per shift and insist she drink. In the morning we would make thin cereal in milk with lavender honey and have her eat.

Over the next three days, Sister Agnès had short periods of wakefulness. Enough that she was able to drink and eat small amounts with assistance several times throughout the day. She drifted in and out of consciousness and was not yet able to sit or stand. When she wet her bed sheets, I was again encouraged. I instructed the Sisters to move and bend her arms and legs three times a day, preferably thirty minutes after she had eaten. Her muscles needed to retain some strength and flexibility; I wanted her on her feet as soon as possible. At the end of the third day, she could squeeze my hands more tightly than the day before and verbally answer yes and no.

Henri had gone to my house after that first long night and brought back with him my horse and wagon. He fed Pedro and the hens and assured them I would be home soon. On the fourth day, the good Sister woke with the sun to smile at us and tell us how foolish we all were to worry so about her. Ah, our Sister Agnès was still herself.

The wound was healing well with no signs of infection and vital signs remained normal. Sister Agnès had gained strength and was now sitting up at the bedside table long enough to slowly eat her meals and converse a bit with the others and myself. In my judgment, she had suffered a moderate concussion, and it would be several weeks or longer before she fully regained use of all her faculties. Based on her reactions and responses, I was confident that she had not suffered a more serious event previous to the fall. Although she did not remember falling, her memory of events before that time remained intact. Her self-deprecating humor regarding her "clumsiness" further assured me that she suffered no long-term issues to her mind.

Henri and Donkey took their leave and headed north at the end of the fourth day. I said my goodbyes the next morning, leaving detailed instructions regarding Sister Agnès's care, which included short, assisted walks about her room every four hours. With hugs all around, I told them I would return in three days. The Sisters sent me on my way with jars of our lavender honey, honey cakes made during those days of nursing, freshly baked loaves of bread, and a basket full of dried meats and cheeses.

I eagerly climbed onto my high wagon perch, and giving Horse his head, we began our walk home. Here atop my wagon seat, my views were unobstructed, allowing me to take in the sights and smells of each changing season. The early winter air was fresh with lingering dampness upon the ground, the birds that stayed through the seasons were waking, and patches of last color lay scattered across the land.

A seat cushion always sat beneath me, as the road was ever bumpy and full of pocks and holes. Horse must have gotten dizzy as he weaved around or between them all, but he knew the way so well I held the reins only to keep my balance during the jostling and dodging. Somehow Horse maintained a steady pace as we made our way—neither fast nor slow.

Nearing home, the familiar poplars along the riverbank began to take form, their branches now nearly bare. The trees were always beautiful to me in any season. The sun moving higher with the day illuminated all that lay ahead, and my breath floated in a mist in front of me. I was becoming chilled and looked forward to laying fresh fires in my stoves.

I experienced that morning a joy beyond any I could remember. Visions, smells, and sounds of life wrapped all around, enfolding me in cleansing renewal. Tears of relief and thankfulness were wet on my face. I could still feel happiness! And recognized that this life I was making was the one I desperately wanted. The suffocating paralysis I had known lifted, replaced by the knowledge that I still had much to offer and much to receive. The seeds had been planted— seeds of abiding friendship and a renewal of self-worth. I was still a competent nurse. I could, even here, even now in this place, tend and heal again. Even more glorious, I had become a part of people's lives, people I cared about deeply and welcomed having them, in turn, care about me. My heart was full as I looked into the morning sun and celebrated this new day's beginning and going home to my house in Meuse.

Back at home, I opened my front door and nearly slipped on a letter that had been pushed beneath it. The sender was Solange, so I opened it quickly, only to find that the letter had actually been written by Papa, the first I had ever received in his own hand. I sat down heavily upon the divan, so startled by this realization and concerned that there was bad news.

They were quite settled now in New York, he wrote, and he went on to describe a life in which both he and Solange were finding great satisfaction. So much so, in fact, that Papa insisted it was time I travel to New York City for a visit in either April or May of this next spring "to experience with them, at least for a visit, our life in America." He went on to write that he was purchasing my ticket, first class, on the SS *Paris*, and Solange would be sending me a trunk of new clothes for the voyage and my stay in New York.

All of the contentment I had experienced just minutes ago seemed to evaporate as I contemplated what might be Papa's intentions for planning, without even inquiring of me, a visit to America. He had sent me off more than two and a half years earlier to find my way alone in Meuse. And now I was to do his bidding again, setting off for another place unknown with no desire to do so?

I felt myself wanting to tear the letter into small pieces and fling it into the cold stove. I wished the letter had gotten lost, never to have arrived to intrude into my life so hard fought for here in Meuse. Did Solange not report to Papa that all was well with me when she visited? We discussed what she would say to him, the reassurances she could convey, that I loved my home, had friends, and felt content and secure. Had she betrayed me? No, not Solange. Not ever.

If Papa had wanted further reassurance he should have paid me a visit himself. But Solange had said that the house held memories for him long put to rest that he did not want to revisit, and that was why he had not traveled with her. We knew he still missed our mothers and had never engaged, as far as we knew, in a relationship with another woman.

Beginning to calm from my frantic pacing as I read and reread the unwelcome letter, I stepped out the front door, taking long deep breaths of the cold November air. Gradually, my heart slowed and my mind resumed a semblance of rational thought. The abiding truth of my life was the unconditional love of my papa and

Solange. I knew all their actions toward me were based on good intentions.

But that knowledge did not preclude my recurring feelings of annoyance, rising up like bile without provocation at Papa's assumptions. Why did he assume I would just leave my home, my animals, my friends, and activities—my life—to take a long voyage on a vast ship wearing clothes I did not choose, with people I did not want to know, and worrying the entire way across the Atlantic as to what awaited me on the other side?

And that was the crux of the matter. What did indeed wait for me in New York City? While I would certainly welcome a reunion with my family, was it worth leaving without fully understanding Papa's intentions for such a visit? My heart began to race again. I decided before I acquiesced to any plans for a visit that I would write to Papa and clearly state the timelines of my stay and my absolute intention to return to my home after three weeks abroad. That any ticket he purchased for me would include my return to France.

In control once more and reassuring myself that I was the one to decide when to go and when to return, I stepped back into my home, my sanctuary, my precious lavender house in Meuse, and set fires to blazing in my stoves.

And then, taking pen to paper, I began my letter to Papa.

CHAPTER 20

LETTER FROM PAPA, DECEMBER 1922

apa's response to my letter arrived a few weeks later. I thought, or probably hoped, that a response would not be forthcoming. That he and Solange would wait upon me to decide whether or not to make the journey, and when I came to a conclusion, I would then communicate to them my intentions.

However, that was not to be. Papa was not a man to wait upon others' intentions, particularly if he felt his own needed further clarification. He had no qualms offering logical persuasion toward what he truly believed was another's correct course of action. Because he truly loved me, his persuasion was sincere in the obvious and stirred my own tenderness towards him.

December 20, 1922

Dear Marie,

As I sit down to respond to your last letter, and to specifically address your concerns regarding a voyage to New York to visit your family, your sister is pacing back and forth behind my back, wringing her hands in fear that I may not adequately clarify my intentions and thereby reinforce your hesitations to undertake such a reunion.

You state in your letter, which I have read multiple times, that you feel I am "summoning" you, perhaps even insisting that you board a ship and sail across the Atlantic because I am "bidding" you to do so. I take it from the tone of your letter that you do, indeed, misread my intentions. Therefore, I do want to provide you with a further explanation for requesting (not summoning, bidding—or dare I say, insisting on) a visit from you.

Does a father not have the right to miss his daughter? You are very far from us yet present and with us in all we do. Your absence is keenly felt. When I would travel, leaving you and Solange at home, I took assurance in the fact that you were well looked after and all your needs were met. Now we are far apart, and I have no such assurances that all is well with you.

Yes, I know what you write, and I read your letters, looking intently for unstated evidence of malcontent, unease, unhappiness, or ill health. And while I have found nothing that would lead me to believe you are not well and thriving in most ways, there is no substitute for sitting across from you, my Marie, and looking into your eyes as you talk to me of your life in Meuse. I want time together without the trappings of your familiar. I want you to leave—to shed for a brief period of time—the cocoon of peace you have carefully spun there in Meuse.

It may be the over-concern of a devoted father for his precious child or a need for me to believe you cannot possibly create an existence of self-sufficiency without my assistance, and while I sincerely hope you are well in all ways, I need to see you for myself. I need to hear in your own voice, your own words what will convince me that setting you upon that train all alone to a place unknown some two years ago was, after all, the right decision. For I have continually questioned that action on my part, wondering if leaving for Meuse was to be your final undoing or your sought-after salvation.

I desperately want to believe that all you write to us is the truth. That you are at peace, that you have found sanctuary in your home, you find your friends kind and thoughtful, and finally, you are again finding yourself busy and needed. I desire nothing more than to be able to lay aside my anxieties over your welfare knowing you are well settled and thriving.

And could I not come to see for myself if what you say is so? Yes, but (and while I did not want to share this trivial concern, Solange insisted I tell you to further clarify our situation), my doctors tell me the small stroke I suffered in 1916 is the reason I now tire more easily than is convenient. Nothing of consequence to keep me from my daily routines, but I am admonished if I overextend myself, and traveling now is something I do just across town. I share this with hesitation as I am feeling entirely well but am complying with your sister and my physician's admonitions in order to keep the peace.

And so, my dearest Marie, I extend to you again a heartfelt invitation to pay us but a brief visit, bringing with you the stories of your life in Meuse. I visualize you there in that serene place surrounded by your expansive fields of purple lavender, as I can still see your mother in those same fields when we journeyed there together so long ago.

Should you acquiesce to a visit, please know that my invitation is based on my hope of seeing you again, to bask in your presence as well as the presence of our family, the three of us together for even a short, precious time.

Your Devoted Papa

While Papa's words were reassuring, they did not truly appease my reticence. I did not fully understand my own apprehensions, but I did understand the import of Papa's request. From his letter I sensed an underlying urgency, a great need for me to join them and for us to be a family again—even for a few short weeks.

Laying aside my own fears, I wrote Papa a quick response asking him to please send my round-trip ticket and the trunk of clothes, assuring him of my sincere feelings of expectation at seeing both himself and Solange in May. It was as much and as little as I could do.

My last thought as I sealed my letter back to Papa brought a smile to my lips. What clothes of fashion and accoutrements would Solange send to outfit me for such a journey on a ship as fine as the *SS Paris*?

I was sure there would be room in that trunk for my own comfortable trousers.

HISTORICAL PERSPECTIVE – BATTLE OF VERDUN

High rates of mortality were experienced in World War I that terminated the lives of ten million people, largely because of "advances" in weaponry including long range rifles, machine and turret guns, tanks and lethal chemical gas fired in shells, and bomb-equipped aircraft and submarines.

The death toll was unexpected and unprecedented. During the Battle of Verdun alone, which began on February 21, 1916 and ended in November 1916, the following statistics have been reported by armies, countries, and historians:

The number of French and German soldiers killed, wounded, or missing in battle: 708,777.

The number of French and Germans soldiers who died in the Battle of Verdun: 305,440.

The number of French and Germans soldiers wounded or missing in the Battle of Verdun: 403,337.

One-tenth of all French soldiers lost in WWI were lost in the Battle of Verdun.

Soldiers on the killing fields of Verdun died at a rate of one death per minute, round the clock, for the almost-ten months of battle.

By 1918, there were 630,000 war widows in France.

The original plan to evacuate the wounded from battlefields such as Verdun by train to hospitals in Paris was short-lived due to the destruction of the rail lines. The soldiers' wounds were often so extensive that any hope of saving their lives meant immediate medical attention and depended on the efforts and skills of the surgeons and nurses in field hospitals set up on the periphery of the battle lines.

Two million Frenchmen were dead by the end of the war. The majority of those killed were young men who had served in the infantry. The government continued, after the war, to strongly encourage women to renew their country by resuming their rightful and proper roles as wives and mothers. This was difficult to achieve in light of the fact that so many men were forever lost, and the children the country wanted women to bear were never to be. This Great War, the War to End All Wars, left nations depleted, devastated European cultures, and, on the souls of the ten million dead, laid the groundwork for World War II.

References

Ian Ousby, *The Road to Verdun* (New York: Random House, 2002)

John Keegan, *The First World War* (New York: Random House, 1999)

HISTORICAL PERSPECTIVE – LAVENDER

Throughout 2,500 years of recorded history, in accounts from the Egyptians, Phoenicians, Romans, and French, lavender has been used extensively and in many creative ways. It has been a part of the mummification process, cleansed and healed wounds and aches throughout time and wars, purified the air, perfumed bodies and homes, and served as an aphrodisiac. Candles, oils, lotions, and ornamentation, in the form of wreaths and arrangements of its stems and flowers, continue to be produced worldwide. Culinary lavender provides us with aromatic and medicinal teas, flavors baked goods, and stimulates our taste buds in salad dressings, cooking oils, sauces, and candies. Its uses are limited only by one's imagination.

Because of the numerous varieties of this hearty plant, cultivation of lavender has long existed in many parts of the world, including New Zealand, Australia, Japan, and throughout Europe, notably in England and France. Lavender has been grown in France for centuries, primarily in the region of Provence where the sunny climate and rocky, well-drained soil of the hills and mountains create the perfect combination for lavender to grow in wild abundance. During the nineteenth century, the oil of lavender was often collected in portable stills brought into the fields at harvest. Increased demand in the 1920s saw the beginning of lavender cultivation develop more formally as a commercial crop, and the harvest was transported to larger permanent stills for processing.

Lavender has a rich and fabled history of positive properties, including the ability of its rich aroma to affect us spiritually. Some, like the fabled Lemurian civilization, believed lavender could transport one to a place of great peace and higher consciousness. Certainly its varietal beauty and fragrance alone cause us to pause and reflect as its presence in our gardens and our homes can stir our memories and, perhaps for you as with me, provide inspiration for a great adventure into the other-known.

HISTORICAL PERSPECTIVE – APICULTURE AND HONEY

As with lavender, honey and the collection of it from honeycombs has been depicted in historical drawings and writings since ancient times. Some of the earliest evidence of the domestication of bees appears by the Egyptians (2422 BCE), and the myriad uses for honey have been depicted in the hieroglyphics of tombs and temples across ancient cultures. Honey was used extensively for both pleasure and medicinal purposes, often as a healing agent in salves and ointments, in cosmetics, and, of course, for the pure enjoyment of its flavor. It was the nectar of Hindu gods, was ingested as part of celebrations and ceremonies by many cultures, and is referenced in the writings of early Sumerians and Babylonians. Moreover, the honey bee was a symbol of royalty for the ancient Romans.

In ancient cultures, hunting and gathering peoples harvested honey from the hives of wild bees found in rocks and trees but in the process of securing the honey often destroyed both the hives and the bees. Beginning in the mid-1770s, the western honey bee (*Apis mellifera),* one of an estimated 20,000 species of wild bees, was domesticated throughout Europe in sustainable hives, made first of straw and then evolving into rectangular structures of cedar, pine, cypress, and sometimes nowadays of polystyrene.

In 1792, blind Swiss naturalist and beekeeper François Huber experimented with "leaf hives" made of wooden frames that were levered together and opened much as the pages or leaves in a book. This allowed for the study of the nature of bees and greatly increased understanding of their hive building and habits.

In the mid-1800s, Lorenzo Langstroth, a pastor in Pennsylvania, developed sustainable hives that incorporated what came to be known as the "bee space." This one-quarter- to three-eighths-of-an-inch space between the comb frames allowed the bees to move freely as well as provided ample room between the combs to keep the frames separate from one other, preventing damage to the combs themselves. Sustainable hives developed on the principles set forth by Huber, Langstroth, Johannes Mehring (inventor of a wax foundation to provide bees something on which to build a honeycomb), and other early apiculture enthusiasts and researchers greatly enhanced the understanding of everything pertaining to bees and preserving bee colonies while allowing for the efficient harvest of honey and wax.

Meanwhile, around the 1860s, an Italian army officer named Francesco de Hruschka developed the hand-cranked centrifugal extractor: individual honeycombs, several at a time, were placed inside a glass container, and by turning the handle and spinning the honeycombs around, the honey was loosened from the combs and would flow into the bottom of the centrifuge's container and out through a spout. Voilà! The industry of commercialized honey and wax production was born and is very much alive today. It thrives across the world in large enterprises, small cottage industries, within the bounds of cities on rooftops, and for anyone who has space enough for a hive or two. Or, as with Marie, by placing hives among hectares of brilliant lavender.

Many varieties of lavender now grace my home gardens, and the summer is filled with their beautiful blossoms alive with scent and bees!

ACKNOWLEDGMENTS

I deeply appreciate all of those who have provided their support, expertise, and encouragement in this journey toward making this book a reality.

Thank you to my friend and SLP colleague, Kelly Fisher. Your compassionate collaboration truly spurred this project forward!

Thank you to my first early readers and dear friends Christine Genuit and Gale Frederick.

My talented sister, Kathleen Noble, has my everlasting gratitude. Your art graces the covers of my books and makes the settings come alive.

Thanks as well to our daughter, Taya Sanderson Gray, who read the initial draft of the manuscript and provided thoughtful insight into the flow and clarity of the story.

Thank you to Ginger Nocera, a friend and fellow writer, for your willingness to review my work as I review yours. How fun to collaborate!

And to my dear friend, Dominique Dailly, who helped with all things French and who is the soul of Solange.

And a heartfelt acknowledgement of gratitude to my gifted editor, Sally Carr. *Merci! Merci!*

And to Terry, my incredibly supportive husband. Your constant encouragement to "go for it" allowed me to do just that and remain true to the truth of my memories!

I sincerely thank you all!

READER'S GUIDE

1. The author states in the "From the Author" section that the story is based on memories of a past life lived as Marie. Have you or anyone you know believed they have lived a past life?

2. Did the "From the Author" section at the beginning of the book influence your overall feelings regarding the story? Did the author's comments cause you to connect more or less with Marie?

3. Do you think the fact that Marie's papa having traveled so extensively during her childhood influenced her decision to seek adventure? If so, how?

4. Marie, Solange, and Papa were a very close-knit family. In what ways are they able to sustain their relationships once they are living in different parts of the world? How is it similar or different to how we nurture and sustain relationships today?

5. Do you think Marie would have made the decision to go to the house in Meuse had Papa not pushed her to do so? How do you imagine her life if she had remained in Marseille?

6. What are your impressions of Henri? Do you think he would have taken such an avid interest in Marie or have had such strong feelings for her if he had not known her mother?

7. In what ways did Laurent's death affect Marie? Has the death of someone you have known and/or loved affected you in ways you did not expect? If so, how?

8. What role do you think the Sisters from the convent played in Marie's life in Meuse? How would you compare their lives with hers?

9. Post-traumatic stress disorder (PTSD) has been called many different names throughout many different wars. PTSD can result from experiencing other traumas besides being involved in wartime though. Have you or anyone you know suffered from PTSD? How has your or their emotional journey compared with Marie's?

10. Do you think Marie's sacrifices and those of other nurses on the battlefronts during The Great War justified the outcome? What of the sacrifices of the opposing forces who lost the war?

11. The women of France strongly believed they had contributed significantly to their country's wartime efforts and many felt confident that after the war laws would be changed to allow women the right to vote; however, the women of France were denied the right to vote until 1944. The women of Italy did not receive the right to vote until 1946, the women of Greece in 1952. Women in the US, England, and Canada were extended the right to vote by 1928. Discuss reasons why it may have taken longer for some European countries to grant the right to vote to women.

12. Many readers have wondered why the story does not include a romantic interest for Marie. Do you think Marie's having a love interest would have added to or distracted from the story?

13. In what ways do you think the multitude of wars throughout history have affected our world? Do you think wars are ever justified or never so? Why or why not?

14. *The Lavender House in Meuse* is the first book in a series. In the sequel *The Passage Home to Meuse*, Marie encounters new acquaintances and develops relationships with people in America and again when she returns to France. Many characters also reappear in the sequel. Have there been people in your life who have had a sustaining presence? If so, how do you think their presence has positively or negatively affected your life journey up to this time?

15. Sometimes, either through our own or other people's choices, or through events out of our control, people move out of our lives and enter our lives. As your life story has unfolded, how much choice have you had regarding the characters who have impacted your life thus far? How will you sustain or change your story as you move into the future?

CPSIA information can be obtained
at www.ICGtesting.com
Printed in the USA
FSHW010501260421
80840FS